IN THE DEATH RING

Nude and weaponless, she fought a man of twice her weight and strength . . .

She was losing. So she attacked. "It is time, dal Nardo!" She saw him stiffen, and set her mind to carry out the plan, no matter what it cost her.

A groin feint; he countered. Stabbing for his eyes she engaged the injured hand, then made full body lunge, as though her rigid fingers could pierce the throat. But her thrust slipped off; his heavy arms locked around her.

She felt ribs grate—could he live long enough to kill her?

BOOK ONE OF THE
RISSA KERGUELEN SAGA

YOUNG RISSA

F.M. BUSBY

BERKLEY BOOKS, NEW YORK

Young Rissa, Rissa ands Tregare, and
The Long View were originally published
in two volumes as *Rissa Kerguelen* and
The Long View. They were also published in
one volumne as *Rissa Kerguelen.*

YOUNG RISSA

A Berkley Book / published by arrangement with
the author

PRINTING HISTORY
Berkley Medallion edition / June 1977
Berkley edition / May 1984
Fourth printing / January 1986

ISBN: 0-425-08505-8

A BERKLEY BOOK ® TM 757,375
The name "BERKLEY" and the stylized "B" with design
are trademarks belonging to Berkley Publishing Corporation.
PRINTED IN THE UNITED STATES OF AMERICA

For Michele

PROLOGUE:

TWENTY-THREE years before Rissa Kerguelen was born . . .

Aged ninety-two, Heidele Hulzein died. Control of the Hulzein Establishment passed to Heidele's parthenogenetic gene-replicated daughter, Renalle.

The bid of United Energy and Transport won the North American election and ousted the Synthetic Foods combine from control of that continent. UET's new Presiding Committee immediately began construction of the controversial Total Welfare Centers.

Near Crater Lake, Oregon, the first known alien spaceship landed. UET pronounced it a hoax, meanwhile sending Committee troops to investigate.

The commanding general followed orders. As soon as he ascertained that the Shrakken lacked faster-than-light communications, he pumped their ship full of cyanide gas. The media reported the aliens' unfortunate susceptibility to Earthly infections.

Within the year UET's laboratories duplicated the Shrakken space drive. Earth—or rather, UET—began interstellar travel. Going always away from the Shrakken worlds, UET found habitable planets and began colonizing—not always with the colonists' consent.

Some ships did not return. Space is vast and light-speed imposes limits, but dissidents spoke of Escaped Ships and of Hidden Worlds. UET halted exploration to guard its holdings against outlaw raids. Such raids were not long in coming.

Twenty-three years after the Shrakken landing, UET moved —massively—against the Hulzein Establishment. Aged eighty-six, Renalle Hulzein fought and died where she had lived, but her daughter Erika—also parthenogenetic, carrying only Renalle's replicated genes—escaped southward. By Renalle's forethought and her own, she salvaged much of the Establishment's assets and a majority of its personnel.

Fourteen days after Renalle Hulzein's life ended, Rissa Kerguelen's began.

YOUNG RISSA

RISSA and her brother—Ivan Marchant, three years older—were born to free parents. David Marchant and Selene Kerguelen, married oldstyle, worked as a Tri-V reporting team. Rissa could not remember a time when she had not watched the Tri-V news, hoping to see them reporting an item from the field. When she did see them, she waved—and took it as a matter of course that when they finished speaking they usually waved back.

She did not know what "condominium" meant, but she knew she lived in one—a massive building of many levels, bounded by streets. One level was for school, but even when she was too young for school, she was never lonely. First there had been the men and women who tended the creche, and later the ones in the Flat-V beside the kitchen—if she needed something she pushed the button and asked for it, and the person talked to her and usually sent or brought it. Occasionally someone came and helped her when she had not asked, so she knew they could see and hear her, regardless of whether she pushed the button. She liked these people well enough. But she loved David and Selene and Ivan and was always glad when they came home from work and from school.

Rissa was five and had begun school herself the day her parents did not come home. Voris Kerguelen, her uncle, came instead. He prepared a meal for her and Ivan—it was past dinnertime—and refused to answer questions until the children ate. Rissa did not protest; she was hungry.

She was wearing a favorite red dress; her long dark hair was in pigtails. Ivan wore green coveralls; when he grinned he showed new front teeth too big for his young jaws. But when Uncle Voris told them what had happened, Ivan grinned no more. He cried instead, and so did Rissa. She also threw up her dinner.

On assignment, covering a Total Welfare Center riot, David and Selene had been taken hostage. When Colonel Osbert Newhausen ordered his Committee troops to gas the entire block-building, they had been killed with the rest. Tri-V had not shown that incident.

One arm around each child, Voris said, "It happens; they knew the risks. Those murderers—there's no safety anymore." His arms tightened. "But don't worry. I'll take care of you."

He stayed the night, sleeping with a child held close on either side. Rissa slept with an arm across his body, holding Ivan's hand.

THE door buzzer, next morning, interrupted breakfast. Voris admitted a stocky, uniformed woman. She brushed unruly graying hair back from her eyes and said, "Welfare Agent Compter. I have a pickup order for two kids—Ivan Marchant and Rissa Kerguelen. These them?"

"Wait a minute! You can't do that—these are my sister's children. I—"

"You're the uncle?" She presented a document. "Here's the pickup—read it and sign it. Or don't, for all I care. Consent isn't legally necessary—just makes it neater."

Voris began a violent motion, then checked it and took the papers. "Hold on a minute, will you, Ms. Compter? I said these children are my sister's. I'm ready and willing to take the responsibility, so your good offices aren't required."

She took back the folder, thumbed through it. "Voris Kerguelen?" He nodded. She shook her head. "You know better than that, Kerguelen. It says here—not married, oldstyle or freestyle—authorized bachelor quarters only, no children allowed. What do you think you're trying to pull here?"

"Damn it, I can *get* married. Or arrange for child care. I—"

"It won't work—the kids aren't yours and you can't afford it. So sign the pickup or don't, but quit holding up my schedule. I'm busy, even if you're not."

Rissa looked from one to the other, not understanding, and began to cry. Ivan came to hold her, and Voris to hold them both. He said, "Compter—can't you give me some time? Schedules—" He shook his head. "Sure—I know. But these are *children*—and Total Welfare is no more than legalized slavery. I can't let you—"

Flat-voiced; "You can't stop me. And watch your mouth, Kerguelen—or you could be next. Total Welfare is an accepted principle; when the government takes over all your debts and responsibilities and provides subsistence, what more can you ask?"

Voris's fists clenched. "Did you ever hear of choice? *That's* what I ask—for these children. In your hands they'll never have it."

The woman sneered, but spoke formally. "As you well know, when Clients are old enough to be sent out to work, their earnings go into their personal accounts. Thrifty Clients who pay off their obligations and achieve a positive balance have the right to buy out at any time."

"If they don't eat! How many ever make it?" He shook his head. "No—the only ones who ever get out are the few who win big in the lottery."

"We can't help it that these people are basically lazy. That's the *reason* for Total Welfare."

"If you say so." He leaned forward. "And how many are on it now? Fifteen percent? Twenty? The way it's growing, you'd think UET wanted *everyone* Welfared."

Without expression she looked at him. "That's not such a

bad idea, Kerguelen—within limits, not bad at all. And the percentage is nearly thirty. Now—are you going to sign or aren't you?''

He held up a hand. "Wait—you pushed me too fast—I wasn't thinking. What about my sister's estate, and her husband's? I'm executor of their wills; surely I'm authorized to use the money for the children's care. So—''

Compter laughed. "Estates? Those two were charged and convicted of helping instigate the riot. Their assets are forfeit.''

"Damn you! I'll appeal that—and sue in the children's name for damages, for their parents' deaths. You'll see—''

"I see you're as reckless as you are ignorant. Do whatever you please—*after* I get these kids to the Center, where they belong.''

Voris squatted to hold both children tightly. "All right. Ivan—Rissa—you'll have to go with Ms. Compter now. But it won't be for any longer than I can help.'' He stood again. "Very well. I'll get their things together—it won't take long.''

"They take nothing.'' She unzipped her tote bag. "Get them out of those clothes, into these jumpsuits and sandals. That's all they need, where they're going.''

Saying nothing, Ivan exchanged his clothing for the shapeless blue-gray garment. Voris undressed Rissa, but as he fastened the jumpsuit, she reached out.

"My pretty dress!'' Voris looked at the woman; she shook her head and put the dress aside. Rissa evaded Compter's reaching hand and ran to a closet; when she turned back to the room, she held a doll. "My dolly—I *need* my dolly.''

"Take it away from her, Kerguelen.''

Voris gestured, entreating. "But a doll—just *one* doll? *Why?*''

"No personal possessions. The others steal them; it causes fights.'' Voris did not move. Compter shrugged and slapped the small girl, then took the doll and tossed it away. Voris started toward the woman; she laughed. "Touch me and you're Welfared—you know that.''

Tears wet Rissa's cheeks. Compter said, "Come on, crybaby.''

"She is not!" Ivan's voice raised. "Don't call her that! She hardly ever cries."

Fists clenched, Voris said, "She's always been . . . a happy child."

"Then she shouldn't have much trouble adjusting. All right—let's go."

Voris crouched before Rissa, hands cupped near his chest. "Rissa? Look, Rissa." She stopped crying and nodded. "Rissa, this is a pretend doll. See how I hold her? Now I'm going to give her to you, and nobody can ever take her away."

He reached out, and Rissa did; and then it was she who held the doll-sized space of air. "What's her name, Uncle Voris?"

"You name her, Rissa."

"All right." She thought. "She's Selene—like Mommy."

Foot tapping, Compter opened the door. Voris kissed both children and let them go. When he would have followed, the woman shook her head. Rissa looked back and saw him standing, gaze downcast. She waved, but he did not look up.

Then the door closed.

FIRST the familiar corridor, then a moving walkway, then an elevator that sank past many levels to a vast, dimly lit space. Rissa and Ivan followed the woman past massive concrete pillars to one of many parked groundcars, and entered it. Compter drove along aisleways and up a spiral ramp to outdoor sunlight.

They rode for a long time, but Rissa paid little heed to what they passed. Softly, under her breath, she hummed—and in her arms she rocked Selene.

The car slowed. Rissa looked outside and saw they were approaching six massive, grouped buildings, each covering a city block, and connected by enclosed overhead bridges. She saw no windows, only blank slabs colored blue-gray, slightly darker than her jumpsuit.

High fences blocked the perimeter streets; a guard checked them through a gate. Compter drove to the second building on the right, parked and took the children inside—through a lobby, along a large hall and then to a smaller one, and into an office.

Behind a desk sat a fat man whose voice wheezed. Before Compter could speak he said, "Wrong place. Admissions—Division Male, Juvenile, Prepube—that's in 7-A. Female, 9-C. Down to your left and—"

"I know how to find the rooms. I've been on other work lately and didn't know they'd moved Admissions."

As though she had thanked him, the fat man waved a hand and said, "Anytime." She nodded and walked out; the children followed.

In another room, Compter handed papers to a slim black woman. She said, "Ivan Marchant. His docket's in order."

Surprising Rissa, this woman smiled. "All right, Ivan—we'll get you a physical exam and have you settled in no time."

Compter's hand on Rissa's shoulder. "Come on."

Rissa pulled away. "No! I have to be with Ivan!" She ran to hug him.

"But you can't, honey," the black woman said. "Boys and girls live in different divisions." Rissa looked at her, made an effort, and did not cry. She kissed her brother and turned to go.

Ivan called after her. "I'll come see you, Rissa. I'll make them let me!" Then she was in the hall, the door closed behind her.

Along the hall, up flights of stairs to another office—the man Compter greeted was thin, pale-faced, and red-haired. Unsmiling, he looked from papers to Rissa and said, "It's all in order." With a nod Compter turned away, giving Rissa no word or look. When she had gone, the man said, "Five, are you? Young enough to adjust. This time next year, you won't know you ever lived anyplace else." Rissa clenched her jaw, thinking, *No! I'll never forget!*—but she said nothing.

A brown-haired woman, plump in white uniform, took Rissa to another room. White uniforms meant doctors and nurses, so Rissa was not surprised to be undressed while the woman looked and listened, touched her with cold instruments, and felt and thumped here and there. When she was dressed again, the woman finished marking a sheet of paper and said, "You'll do." She called a younger woman in. "Take her up to Dorm Eighteen, will you, Theda? Is she in time for dinner there?"

Theda took papers in one hand and Rissa's hand in the other. "I think so. I'll see that she gets something." They walked out; an elevator took them up several floors to an anteroom that led to a larger room filled with cots. The woman sat and typed on a small card. "This is your nametag. Can you read your name? We'll put it on the head of your cot."

"I can read."

"Good." She patted Rissa's head. "Now sit here a minute and then we'll assign you a bed and go get you something to eat." Rissa sat. Theda opened a drawer and brought out an electric clipper. "Hold still now." And very quickly she clipped Rissa's hair—not to bare scalp, but closely. "All right; let's go."

Rissa's head felt cool; she put her hand to it and felt the short growth, at the borderline between bristle and softness. She did not look at the wastebasket, where Theda had dropped the two long pigtails.

She followed the woman past rows of cots and saw her nametag affixed to one, then to a dining hall filled with long tables. Other small girls in jumpsuits ate silently at those tables. Rissa looked at them; their clipped heads, ears seeming to protrude, were ugly to her. Then, in a polished metal tray, she saw her own reflection.

Theda filler her tray and sat her at a table. "You'll be all right now; the other girls will show you where everything is." And the woman left. Rissa sat, staring at the tray so that she would not have to look at anything else.

She did not eat; she was concentrating totally on not crying. The girl next to her whispered, "Aren't you hungry? You'd better eat." She shook her head, and the other girl quickly exchanged her empty tray for Rissa's full one.

After the meal Rissa followed the others' lead—putting her tray with theirs, following when some visited the washroom and, although she thought she knew the way, back to the dormitory and her own cot. There she lay, saying nothing, staring at the ceiling until the lights were extinguished.

Only then, in the dark, she turned on her side and curled up into the smallest, tightest space she could manage. Holding her head in both hands she cried herself to sleep.

THE Center was a simple world; Rissa's first day set a pattern for the endless time that followed. Dormitory Eighteen was one of many, each housing forty girls aged four to twelve. The older ones told the younger what to do and brusquely helped them when necessary; Rissa saw few adult supervisors.

Thrice a day she was fed. After breakfast she was first instructed and then given practice in such skills as scrubbing blue-gray walls and brown floors. After lunch she was free to play in the bare gymnasium or watch Tri-V in the auditorium. She liked Tri-V because nowhere else did she see printed words; she had been reading for a year and was proud of the ability. She was less fond of the play group because there some of the older girls bossed the younger ones, teasing them or forcing them into unwelcome competitions. When one such, from a different dormitory, tried to coerce Rissa, she ran away and shunned the gymnasium for several days. When she did return, the other paid her no attention.

After dinner, when the dormitory lights had gone dark, Rissa lay wrapped in her one blanket on the plastic mattress. It was then, before she went to sleep, that she cuddled and crooned softly to Selene, the pretend doll that Voris had given her.

EVERY seventh day, after lunch, her dormitory group left jumpsuits on the cots and marched down the hall to showers.

YOUNG RISSA

Before every fourth shower, the forty girls waited in line for their hair to be clipped to short plush.

TWICE, Voris visited her. The first time she was called to the anteroom to meet him, he dropped to his knees, hugged her and cried, repeating her name. Then he said, "I don't know how long it's going to take—the lawsuit to get you and Ivan out of here. The government—it's stalling, of course—is looking for grounds to Welfare *me*. If I don't come back sometime, you'll know they've succeeded." He blinked tears away and smiled. "But that won't kill the lawsuit, honey—my lawyer's tied it in with nearly a hundred others, on a class-action basis."

She did not understand, and asked only, "Where's Ivan?"

"Only one building away—Division Male, Juvenile, Pre-pube. I saw him, Rissa; I just came from there. He says to tell you he loves you."

"Tell him I love *him*, too!"

"I already did."

"Why can't I *see* him?"

"I've asked, but they stalled me. Next time I'll ask again." They talked a little longer. He said, "Do you still have . . . Selene?"

She smiled. "Oh, yes! I do—and thank you, Uncle Voris!"

He kissed her and left. Her days continued as before; she did not see Ivan, nor hear of him. When Voris came again, she had almost forgotten that there was such a thing as the outdoors—but only almost, for she tried very hard to remember all that she could. And each night before sleep came, she repeated to Selene as much as she could recall.

This time she sat on Voris's lap. When she asked of Ivan, he said, "They wouldn't let me see him. Said he was in punishment status, whatever that means. They wouldn't say, but it can't be too serious—he's only eight. Next time—" Then, in a voice that raised prickles on Rissa's spine, he said, "There's a name—I'm going to tell you, and you must never forget. Newhausen—Colonel Osbert Newhausen. Rissa—can you remember?"

She frowned. "Newhausen?" She was no longer sure of her memory. "Just a minute, Uncle Voris." She jumped down, ran to the dormitory, and brought back the nametag from her cot. "Write it down for me? On the back of this?" He took the card; she saw him print the name carefully. She repeated it and said, "Why do I have to remember that?"

"This is the man who killed your mommy and daddy—Selene and David—so that you were put in here, and Ivan where he is." Voris sighed. "Rissa—it's a lot to ask of a little girl. But if I and the others fail—perhaps someday you'll get the chance to pay him back for all of it." She was not sure she understood but unsmiling, she nodded.

When he left she returned the nametag to its place, and that night she told Selene about Colonel Osbert Newhausen. "You have to help me remember, Selene—will you?"

Voris did not come again, nor did she see Ivan. She asked older girls about seeing her brother, and then an adult supervisor who told her, "I don't have the authority. Mr. Croutch does."

Rissa nodded. "All right. Can I ask him?"

"He doesn't come here."

"Then how—?"

"I'll put in the request for you. But don't expect anything."

RISSA ate and slept, worked and played and watched Tri-V, and at dark she talked to Selene. Her jumpsuit wore out and became too small; she was issued a larger one. By accident she learned a way to touch herself so as to feel excited, and then relaxed; every night, after she told Selene goodnight, she did this.

Some of the girls, she saw, had friends. But Rissa had never had any friend but Ivan.

YOUNG RISSA

• • •

IN the windowless Center, Rissa knew no seasons; time passed uncounted. One afternoon in the gymnasium she wrenched her ankle and limped back to lie on her cot alone. She was dozing when the new chief supervisor, a middle-aged woman, brought in a small, crying girl. Rissa sat up, yawning. The woman said, "Can you take care of this one for a while?" And, as Rissa nodded, "What's your name? How old are you?"

"Rissa Kerguelen. I'm five."

The woman shook her head. "You're older than that."

"No—my last birthday, I was five. I remember."

"But—oh, never mind. Here—take this kid—talk to her or something. Somebody's scared her." The woman turned away, then looked back. "You're a hell of a lot older than five; I know that much."

When the woman was gone Rissa considered the crying child—small, with big ears and a thin face below the freshly clipped blonde hair. She ran her hand over the plushlike texture and tipped the little girl's face up to look at her.

"I'm Rissa. What's your name?"

The child gulped, hiccupping. She shook her head. "I want Ladygirl!" Again she cried. Rissa drew the small form to her—clasping, cuddling, putting the head to her shoulder and stroking it.

"Who's Ladygirl?"

"My best dolly—they said—they said I could have her!"

Remembering, Rissa thought, *they lied to her, to keep her quiet until they got her here. That's even worse than . . .*

She shifted the child off her lap and sat her on the cot, turned to face her. "Look," she said, and placed her arms and hands to hold Selene. Back and forth she rocked Voris's gift.

"What are you doing . . . Rissa?" Then; "I—I'm Elena."

"All right, Elena." She continued rocking. "Now maybe Ladygirl can't get here for a while—you see? But right here—" She patted Selene's head. "—I have a pretend doll.

Her name's Selene. My uncle Voris gave her to me, and nobody can ever take her away from me." Elena's eyes were huge. Rissa thought, *I know it's only pretend—but I can't give Selene away!* So she said, "Would you like to hold her for me?" Elena nodded. Rissa moved to make the transfer. "Be careful, now—don't drop her."

"I won't." Carefully Elena held air as though it were substance. Rocking, she crooned to what she held. Her voice sounded sleepy.

Rissa spoke. "Why don't you take a nap with her? You don't have a cot yet, do you?" Elena shook her head. "All right; you can use mine."

Soon Elena slept. When the supervisor came in, Rissa put finger to lip. The woman nodded and beckoned. Limping not so much now, Rissa followed to her office.

"I see you handled her all right; thanks. Here's her nametag; pick any vacant cot you like." Rissa nodded. "Now, then, sit down." She sat. "What's the idea of telling me you're only five years old? I looked it up—you're eight, almost nine."

Rissa shook her head. "No. How could I be? I haven't had any birthdays, and—"

"Of course you've had birthdays! Three of them, since you came here."

"Nobody ever told me . . ."

Eyes narrowed, the woman said, "Why, you're telling the truth, aren't you?" And frowning now, "I'm new here—I don't know all the problems—but that's ridiculous. It *can't* be all that much extra work to keep track of the dates so you kids could sing 'Happy Birthday' for each other. I'll put it up to the Director." She paused. "What happens here at Christmas? Anything?"

"No—there isn't any Christmas here, I think."

"Hmmm—well, maybe I couldn't swing that one; funds *are* short. But I'll ask." She stood and held out her hand; Rissa rose and grasped it. "I'm Natalie Kimbrough. Anything you want to know, come and ask me."

"Could—can I see my brother Ivan? I haven't, since . . ."

"Ivan Kerguelen? How old is he?"

YOUNG RISSA

"Ivan Marchant. He's—he was eight when I was five."

"Do you know your birthdays?"

Rissa shook her head. "No. I did, but I forgot."

"Then he could be either Prepube or Postpube by now. I'll check, and let you know."

"Thank you, Natalie Kimbrough. Uh—should I go now?"

"All right—no, wait a minute. You're old enough to be helping with the younger ones. Have you been?"

"No. Not much, anyway."

"Why haven't you? You seem to be good at it."

Rissa shrugged. "I just—I don't talk a lot, I guess."

"I see. Well—will you take care of little what's-her-name?"

"Elena? All right."

"Good. Okay—maybe you'd better hop to it now." And as Rissa left, for the first time she smiled at a Welfare supervisor.

SHE affixed Elena's nametag to a vacant cot near her own and turned to find the child awake, watching her. "Here's your cot. I put your name on it—see?"

A nod. The little girl rose, still holding Selene, and moved to her place. Rissa thought, and said, "Here—I'll have to put Selene back now, where she's used to sleeping." Elena whimpered, and Rissa said, "—but you can have her *sister*." The small girl quieted. "Here—let me put Selene to bed before she wakes up and cries. Then I'll bring you, uh—"

"*Who*, Rissa?"

"Oh! We haven't named her yet. She's very young." Rissa pantomimed the taking, the laying down of one, then the picking up and transfer of the other. "What would *you* like to name her?"

Brows wrinkled above Elena's small face. "I think—Ladygirl!"

"But—" Then Rissa realized that Elena *knew*. She said no more.

● ● ●

RISSA adopted Elena as her charge, and suddenly found herself talking more with other girls of her own age and older, mostly in regard to their young wards. It was from a twelve-year-old, suddenly transferred to Postpube, that she informally inherited small Marie. Marie, dark and chubby, seemed content to be Elena's shadow; Rissa was equally content to leave it at that.

In the dining hall Natalie Kimbrough hung a large page-per-day calendar; onto each child's nametag she stuck a tiny replica of the appropriate birthday page. Few could read but all could memorize the sticker and recognize, at breakfast, the calendar page that matched it. Each girl had the responsibility of announcing her own birthday, so as to be sung to by the rest at dinner.

In Natalie Kimbrough's office: "Rissa—about your brother —I tried, but no permission. First, he's in Postpube; that makes it tougher. Worse, every time I ask he's in punishment or on probation and can't have visitors—or messages, even. I'm afraid the boy isn't doing too well."

"But if I could see him—I could *tell* him, don't do things and get punished. I—"

"I know—but that's not the way they work it here."

ONE morning, short of Rissa's own birthday, the calendar was gone. She went to Natalie Kimbrough's office; a stranger greeted her.

"Kimbrough? She's not here any more. A troublemaker, she was. But I'm putting a stop to all that." The woman scowled. "And what did *you* want with her?"

Rissa thought fast. *Troublemaker?* "I—I was just supposed to report whether Elena and Marie were getting over their colds. They are—they're fine now."

"All right. You—whatever your name is—get back to work."

Rissa went. And now again, as before the time of Natalie Kimbrough, she stayed well clear of the supervisor's office.

YOUNG RISSA

• • •

But she could now, after a fashion, count time. She could name the months and knew how many days made a year. She stole a pencil—her very first theft—and along the inside of her cot's frame she listed months and days.

She knew her calendar was not exact. She was not sure which months were longer; to fill out her year, she assigned them thirty days or thirty-one at random. And she was uncertain of the exact time-lapse between the loss of the large calendar and the beginning of her own—five days? Eight? She settled for a week and began from there.

But *her* year did not run January-to-December. She began it with her birthday. And since she had forgotten the date of Christmas she put it at the end of her year, giving her two consecutive personal holidays to share with Elena, Marie, Selene, Ladygirl and—Marie's pretend doll, Selene's *other* sister—Samantha.

So when Rissa first bled—her breasts as yet hardly noticeable—she knew she was eleven, nearly twelve. She also knew she must report the occurrence or be punished when it was discovered. She was frightened because girls who bled were taken to Postpube and did not return, even to visit. But no one had said they were punished, so—after saying good-bye to her two young friends and seeing them safely in charge of another girl—she went to the chief supervisor.

She pointed to her stained jumpsuit. "I've started."

He nodded, unsmiling, and rose. "Come with me."

"My papers?"

"I'll see to them. And you don't need to return to the dormitory; you own nothing there." So she followed him, down corridors and up stairs she had never seen, to a door marked "Surgery."

Inside the first room—green walls, a carpet on the floor—behind a desk sat a woman with unclipped hair. She looked at Rissa. "Tubal ligs, right? All over before it begins."

"Probably. But this one—I checked—she's named in that old recovery lawsuit. So use the magnetic sections, just in case. Not much chance, of course, but there's no point in giving the Underground any more to make a stink about, than we can help."

The woman snorted. "All right, if you say so. You sign the authorization, though. *I'm* not financing any reversibles."

Rissa understood none of it. The supervisor left; the woman took her to another room. Soon she was on a table with a cone over her face, fighting to breathe. When she woke, her belly hurt.

She lay on a cot in a strange dormitory, almost like the one she knew except that the cots were larger. And so were the girls—some of them she knew from before. So she knew she was in Section Female, Juvenile, Postpubertal.

She remembered the tall, pale girl—Sandra?—yes—who came to stand by her bed. "Rissa, isn't it? Hadn't expected you so soon. How you feeling?"

Rissa touched the blanket over her belly. "It hurts. What did they do?"

"You're sterilized, that's all. Like the rest of us."

"What's sterilized? Why do they—"

"So we won't ever have babies. They cut out something so we can't. Too many of us already, they say."

"Oh." As Sandra walked away, Rissa thought, *I didn't want any babies anyway—not in here. And I don't need any. I've got—*

But she hadn't! Now she realized—she had left Selene on her old cot! She formed her arms into cuddling embrace and whispered, "It's pretend—she can be *here*, just as easy." But no matter how she willed it, there was no Selene. Nor could she now conjure a substitute.

Fatigue overcame her. Before sleep, her last thought was: *Whoever gets my cot, I hope she'll know Selene's there—and be good to her. . . .*

YOUNG RISSA

• • •

HER belly's soreness eased; the bandages came off. She was left with minor scarring, and gradually it faded to whiteness.

She had lived with children; now she was among adolescents. And adult supervisors were more in evidence. Emil Gerard, chief supervisor in Postpube, was a fattish man. He smiled a great deal, but the smile did not reach his eyes or voice.

She learned new tasks. Among them, once a week she dusted Gerard's office, early in the morning before he arrived. In that office were wall and desk calendars—she discovered and corrected the errors in her own. Her accumulated discrepancy, she found, was only six days.

Some things here differed from Prepube. Not many girls used this gymnasium. Rissa did not mind—she liked to run, and here she had more room and fewer obstacles.

Missing Selene's solace she needed others to talk to, and became less solitary. Sandra, fat Eloise, a black girl named Delia—these came to be, if not friends, her closest acquaintances. The four shared rumor and gossip and minor conspiracies against Authority—such as smuggling tidbits from dinner for late snacks.

One night Sandra came to Rissa's cot. "Let me show you something," she began to touch Rissa in the way Rissa liked to touch herself. "Have you done this before?"

"Only by myself."

"Do it to me, too." Rissa did. After a time, Sandra stopped. "That's enough. Wasn't it good?"

"I guess so. But not like it is when I do it myself."

"Oh. Well, here—maybe *this* is better." But to Rissa it was not. And when the next night's attempt also failed, Sandra did not try again.

• • •

RISSA was fourteen when the epidemic struck. She was one of the last to succumb. Several had died, she knew, so the illness terrified her. Fever racked her, and delirium; she dreamed of horror and was not sure of reality. Once she thought she saw Gerard and heard him ask an attendant, "This one—you think she'll live?"

"I doubt it, sir. She's pretty bad."

"That's all. You can go." The other left; Gerard locked the door and pulled a screen to shield Rissa's cot. Then he removed his garments and climbed atop Rissa—and now she knew it was real enough. He angered her so with pain that she set her mind and refused to die.

When she recovered and next saw Gerard she feared his look. "How are you feeling?" he said. "Stronger?"

"Yes. But I cannot remember anything—except such terrible dreams." He nodded and turned away, and then she felt safer.

Now she was old enough to be sent outside, carrying a date-stamped Welfare pass, to work. The first day, waiting with her group, she listened carefully. The speaker, a Client from Section Female, Adult, began, "Most of you are new so I'll tell you the rules. First, stay with the group and do *not* lose your passes. Or your lunchbags—our employers don't feed us and it's a long haul from breakfast to dinner. If you ever do get lost, ask the nearest freeperson to call the number marked on your pass. You'll be picked up—and punished, of course, enough so you'll be more careful next time."

Her lopsided grin lacked humor. "Anyone who's thinking of running away—and hell, I *know* some of you are—forget it." She touched her head, then her jumpsuit. "There's no refuge on this continent for Welfare haircuts and Welfare clothes. And when you're brought back, you're *really* punished."

She looked back and forth across the group, keeping her gaze on someone to Rissa's left. "Anytime I give this talk, I can spot the smart ones. You're thinking; steal a wig, steal a dress. Sure—it's been done. Steal some money, even—right? But where are you going to steal a freeperson's ID with *your* fingerprints on it, sealed in plastic?" She shook her head. "No—don't try it. I'm no Welfare toady—I hate this place and make no secret of it. That's why you can believe me when I say there's no way out. Because if there were, *I'd* be out."

Rissa did not hear the question, but the woman's answering laugh held even less humor than her grin. "The Underground? I wouldn't know. I tried to get in contact with it—never mind why. That's what put me in here—turned out I was talking to an undercover Committee agent instead.

"All right; the bus should be ready. Let's go."

The work, that day and most later ones, was scrubbing, washing—any task freepersons would not perform for the pittance Total Welfare charged. Working outside had advantages —Rissa knew that each day meant a small credit to her Welfare account. And she enjoyed seeing different places, outside the Center—and morning and evening, from the bus, the almost-forgotten outdoors!

There was one disadvantage. In the Center her afternoons were free. Outside work occupied the entire day.

She did not go every day. Employers' demands varied, and when fewer workers were needed they were chosen at random or—sometimes—allowed to volunteer. Rissa's choice, when given it, depended on how recently she had had a free afternoon. But the occasional change of routine helped relieve monotony.

ONE morning Gerard summoned her. "I need more singles." Not understanding, Rissa said nothing. "Girls to go work by themselves, not in groups." She nodded. "I hear you're a good worker—no trouble. The problem is, we give you a pass on public transit, but how much of the city do you know? How much information do you need, to be able to find an address?"

"If you could show me on a map . . ."

"That's no good. We'd have to teach you to read first."

She shook her head. "No. I can read."

"Oh, a few words, I suppose—off the Tri-V. But *really* read? There's no way you could have learned that."

"I always could. From before I was here, I mean."

He leafed through some papers, chose one and handed it to her. "Here. Read that to me." Stumbling over a few unfamiliar words, she did so. He took the paper back.

"You should have told someone—you could be doing more valuable work. Come with me; we'll have to test you."

She followed him down two levels to a small, brightly colored office. There a short Oriental man heard Gerard's instructions. "Test the reading level and general intelligence. She can't know any math, but she might have the aptitude. We're too short of help to waste brains with any kind of head start." The man nodded and Gerard left.

"Sit down, please. I'm Doctor Otaka. And you are . . . ?"

"Rissa Kerguelen."

"Age? And how long have you been in Welfare?" She told him; he began to ask another question, then said, "No, never mind—that's all in your file. Gerard forgot to bring it, but I can check later." He smiled—a real smile—Rissa remembered Natalie Kimbrough.

He said, "Reading level, eh? A rare request these days. What else can you do? Anything with numbers?"

"I can—I can add and subtract. I used to know how to multiply, but I forgot. I was just starting to learn division when they came and took me—took me and Ivan . . ."

"Ivan?"

"My brother. They've never let me see him. Could you—"

He shook his head. "Not a chance. Last year, maybe. But the new chief in Division, Male, is a real pile—with barnacles!

"Now, then." He shoved papers at her, and a pencil. "Can you read the directions all right?"

She looked. "Yes."

"Then go ahead. Starting—*now*."

Not quite understanding the purpose but willing to oblige,

she read, wrote, read and wrote again. When she was done, Otaka said, "You're fast. Finished with three minutes to spare. Now, then—do you know what an intelligence test is?"

She thought. "When I was four—matching patterns, putting pegs in holes."

"Well, this one is a little different."

And it was. Written questions, each with five answers from which to choose. Some she did not understand at all; some she comprehended vaguely; many were clear to her. At last she said, "I don't think I can answer any more of it. Was I fast again?"

He smiled. "Yes, somewhat. And now it's time for lunch."

"All right. I can find my way there. Should I come back? Is there any more you want me to do?"

He looked at his watch. "Actually, it's past time to eat at your dining room."

She shrugged. "It doesn't matter. I've missed lunch before —I'm not *very* hungry."

"No, no! We'll have no work on empty stomachs. I intended, anyway—you'll lunch with me in the staff dining room."

Dubiously, "I don't think they'll like that."

"I'm conducting tests and you're my subject—enough said. Come along."

She did, and although uneasy in the strange circumstance, enjoyed the food, the unfamiliar variety and flavors. The meat and some vegetables were quite new to her, but she asked no questions.

Afterward, again in Otaka's office, he said, "Would you mind doing a few more series? I'd like to establish a psychological profile."

"I don't know what that means, but all right."

"Well, I'm studying the effects of the Welfare environment, especially on children." He smiled again. "That's not much better, is it? Let's just say I'm trying to learn about people and I'd like you to help me. But you don't *have* to—this is my own idea, not Gerard's orders."

"Sure. Sure—I'll help *you*." And it was a long three hours

before Rissa was done with the succession of tests. When she left, what most surprised her was the doctor's handshake as he said good-bye.

WHEN Gerard next called her he said only, "You're too smart for scutwork. You're going to save me some money." He turned to the woman at a smaller desk, a woman whose hair was unclipped and who wore a bright dress. "Rissa, this is Elva Sommrech, my aide. Elva, as soon as you teach Rissa enough to handle your desk, you're free to take that promotion over in Prepube."

Sommrech's high-arched eyebrows disappeared under heavy brown bangs. "A little for me, a lot for you? Oh, no, Emil—I want a percentage! How about a third?"

Gerard frowned. "In *private*, Elma!"

"What's the difference? She'll have access to the records —and see you have her coded as paid staff, not as a Client." She shook a finger at him. "I want my cut."

He shrugged. "I don't pay blackmail. If the promotion isn't enough for you, we'll drop the whole thing."

After a frowning pause, Sommrech grinned. "What the hell—it was worth a try. Excuse me a minute, then I'll start the girl's training."

When she was gone, Gerard said, "And if *you* get any fancy ideas, it's back to scrubbing floors." He glared at Rissa. "*Do* you?"

She shook her head. He was cheating her but she could not protest. His cheating of the State did not concern her. But— *access to the records!*

IN the next weeks, Elva Sommrech taught her the uses of keypunch and readout machines, the Center's coding system and the access codes to other Sections' data banks. Rissa learned procedures for entering new Juvenile Clients, routines for keeping their daily records, and how to transfer them at sixteen to Section Female, Adult. Some menial chores she still performed; now each morning she went early to tidy and dust the office. When both her superiors arrived, she was allowed thirty minutes to go to breakfast. Then her training continued.

One morning Sommrech did not appear. Gerard told Rissa, "The job's all yours now." He locked the office door. "There's one part Elva couldn't teach you. Take off your jumpsuit and bend over the desk."

At first she felt some pain, then only discomfort, and at the end a brief flash of unsatisfied excitement. Then he withdrew and said, "Wipe yourself off and go get your breakfast."

Slowly she dried herself and got into her jumpsuit. "Do I have to do that every day?"

"Yes. And you're not to tell anyone. Understand?"

She nodded and left. On her way to breakfast she thought, *He's not supposed to do that. But it's better than scrubbing floors.* And now she knew why he had wanted her out of the office for a half hour each morning.

IN her work she learned much. Accustomed to the idea that Authority got what it wanted, rules or no rules, she was not surprised to discover the ways Gerard used to divert Center and Client moneys to his own use. She despised the dishonesty; her early training recoiled against it. But, scrubbing floors again? She decided she could only lose by any protest. To Gerard, of course, she pretended ignorance.

Her computer terminal, she knew, recorded the placement —but not the content—of any request for data outside her own Section. So despite her anxiety, she waited.

Then came a request from Doctor Otaka, for correlative data from Section Male, Juvenile, Postpubertal and Section Male, Adult—and at last she could punch inquiry on Ivan Marchant! He'd be seventeen, she thought—Male, Adult. Frowning, she punched the codes.

Of the readout, she understood little. "Standard measures against recalcitrance" was a frequent entry and recently increasing. She tried to think of a way to see her brother, but could not; "visiting regulations" were a system of prohibitions, not permissions. So she memorized his individual code number—which would give access to his file without recording her call—noted his location, and destroyed the telltale readout segments. She would have to wait.

OTHERWISE, Rissa did not brood on her way of life. She worked, ate, slept, ran before dinner in the gymnasium, and operated her various office machines. She considered Gerard to be one of them; his morning demands no more unpleasant than cleaning the photocopier. Except that on the days she bled, the hard floor hurt her knees.

Evenings, sometimes, she still watched the Tri-V—but saw it as fantasy, for the lives it showed were quite unlike her own. Vaguely she recalled having looked and dressed like the children the screen showed, but came to think the memories must be false or derived from prior viewing.

With mixed feelings she awaited her sixteenth birthday and transfer to Section Female, Adult. Rumors gave her a dull dread. But despite herself she could not suppress a wild, reasonless spark of hope.

During her last weeks before transfer a blonde woman—Gerda Lindner, staff, not Client—worked with Rissa, training to take over the work. Rissa wondered whether the other would also have to bend over the desk each morning, and if so, whether she knew it yet.

THE morning she reported not for work but for transfer, she found Gerard alone. Tight-lipped, pale, he paced the floor.

"Now listen fast," he said. "You're going out of Welfare, I

suppose, and I have to make you understand that you *can't* talk about the Center, outside. You see—"

"Out of Welfare?" Never had she interrupted Gerard. "How?"

"The lottery, how else? Just a few minutes ago, it was announced on Tri-V. The top prize—awarded six months in a row to ineligibles, unclaimed and piling up—and the damned ticket's *in your name*. You—"

She stopped hearing him. She knew that Gerard bought lottery tickets with Juvenile Clients' work-credits. Losses cost him nothing. Winnings, payable to the Client at transfer time, were Gerard's meanwhile, to invest for his own profit.

But one of "her" tickets had won, and it *was* transfer time. So, with the media watching, *she would buy out of Welfare!*

Dazed, she asked, "The big one?" Then; "How much?"

"The newsies weren't sure. Even after taxes, though— millions of Weltmarks."

"Taxes? On State money, awarded by the State?"

"Of course. All income is taxable."

In Gerard's presence, until now, she had not laughed. "I see. They take money out of one pocket and put it in the other, so they can say the prize is bigger than it really is." She shook her head. "Never mind—so long as it buys me out of here." She looked at him, wondering if she had said too much. "What happens now?"

Gerard cleared his throat; when he spoke, his voice showed strain. "The press is coming. To talk to you before you leave. You mustn't—just say you're very happy, and grateful to the State, and you wish everyone could be as lucky as you are. Or else—"

"Or else . . . trouble?" Suppressing what she felt, again she shook her head. "I will speak nicely to the press about my life here."

His smiled showed relief. "Good. I've ordered up some clothes and a wig, so you'll look better on Tri-V for the home folks."

Before she could stop herself; "The hell with the home folks!" Then, quickly, "Wait a minute—I said I wouldn't *say* anything. But I won't look a lie, Gerard." For the first time she called him by name. She felt surges of life, energy, power, but she was not yet free of this place. She fought them down and smiled. "I'm sure the public knows a Welfare haircut when it sees one. There's no point in pretending lottery winners get that much advance notice. That's all I meant."

With clenched fists he thumped the desk. "All right, all right—forget the wig. But wear the clothes, won't you? I mean, you *are* buying out of Welfare. Why give the appearance that you're not?"

She thought. "Yes, that's reasonable—if the clothes are. I mean, nothing fancy or expensive-looking."

"Not likely—the stores aren't open yet. Gerda's rounding up some things in your size, from some of the live-in staff."

"Yes. Will she be here soon? And when do the newspeople arrive?"

"Shouldn't be long now. Half an hour, maybe, until your interview." He looked at her. "Rissa? You're one of the best girls I've had here. Would you—?"

She knew his intent and answered it. "No. Because never before—not even once—did you *ask* me. You always just told me."

A knock cut off whatever he might have said. Blonde Gerda entered, carrying clothing and a curly reddish wig. "Here you are, Gerard—and you, you lucky darling! Here—let me fix you up all pretty for the camera."

Rissa shook her head. Gerard said, "Forget about pretty—she won't wear the wig and knows nothing of makeup. Just get a dress on her—and for God's sake, hurry!"

THE red dress fit poorly, but Rissa would wear no other. Unfamiliar with underclothing, she refused it. Gerard sent Gerda for a suitcase; when she returned, she packed the rest of the clothes and the wig.

"Here you are, kid; it's all yours." The woman left momentarily; a few seconds later, she opened the door again. "The press is here. Tell it like you believe it."

YOUNG RISSA

• • •

To Rissa's surprise, Gerard carried the suitcase. In the auditorium the Tri-V was turned off, and instead of jump-suited girls the chairs were filled with outsiders—the press, waiting to interview the winner of one of the largest lottery prizes ever won.

Standing beside the darkened Tri-V, facing the cameras, she waited while Gerard introduced her—name, age, parentage and provenance. Then the questioning began.

"What's your reaction to winning the big prize?"

"Naturally, I'm delighted."

"How does it feel to grow up in a Welfare Center?"

"I can't answer that; I've never grown up anywhere else. How does it feel to grow up outside?" Laughter.

"The last big winner called it an utter miracle. Do you agree?"

"No." She shrugged. "Why should I? Every month, as long as I can remember, it happens—with the winners announced on Tri-V. This time it's me, is all."

A moment's silence. "Who will you vote for in the next election?"

"I don't understand."

"Which bidding conglomerate has your support?"

"I can't say—I don't know enough about any of them."

"Does that mean you don't favor the present Committee?" She bit her lip. "It doesn't mean *anything*, yet. Give me time to learn."

From the rear, a harsh voice. "You better learn fast, kid."

A gray-haired woman spoke. "What do you intend to do with the money you've won? And with your life, from now on?"

Rissa thought. "Buy my brother out of Welfare—my uncle Voris, too, if he's still alive—and share with them. That's the money." She smiled. "My life? Well, I'm going off Earth and I'm going to grow my hair down to my butt—and the rest of it's my own business."

Gasps, then the same woman asked, "You resent your present hairstyle?"

"What's to resent? A few sets of clippers are a lot cheaper than combs and brushes always getting lost and wearing out; anybody can see that. I don't have to like it, though, and I never did."

"What are you going to do, off Earth?"

"I don't know yet. What are *you* going to do, *on* Earth?"

As the newspersons packed their equipment and began to leave, Gerard said, "Come with me. There's a pogiecopter waiting on the roof pad." This time she carried her own suitcase.

On the roof, besides the copter and its pilot they found the gray-haired newswoman. She said, "If I may, Rissa, I'd like to ride with you. Where are you going?"

"She's booked into the Sigma-Hilton," said Gerard, "until she arranges for permanent quarters. But you had your interview with the rest—isn't this a little unethical?"

"I'm not here as a reporter; I'm a friend of the family." She turned to Rissa. "I doubt you'll remember me; you were very young. I'm Camilla Altworth."

Rissa thought, then smiled. "Yes—my father bringing in the mail—he'd say 'We have a letter from Camilla.' They'd read it, and laugh and talk—and my mother would write to you the very same day. No, I don't remember actually seeing you, but—yes, do come with me. You can tell me about David and Selene—things I've forgotten, or never knew."

Gerard cleared his throat. "Well, I guess it's all right. You'd better get aboard; you're keeping the pilot waiting." He held out his hand. "Good-bye, Rissa."

She looked at the hand, then nodded and took it. *After all, he could have been worse.* "Good-bye, Gerard."

"Til we meet again."

"We won't." She climbed inside; Camilla Altworth followed.

YOUNG RISSA

• • •

THE lazy pogiecopter took them to the roof pad atop the Sigma-Hilton. Below, at the desk, Camilla Altworth took charge, but when she gave Rissa's name, the man smiled and said, "It's all arranged. Will you be staying also, as Ms. Kerguelen's guest?"

The woman looked at Rissa. Rissa said, "Maybe; we'll see."

A bellman took them to a three-room suite. Impressed by the lush decor, Rissa waited until he left, to say, "Camilla, isn't it beautiful?"

"For its time, yes. About thirty years out of date, though." Then, "Oh, hell—I've hurt your feelings. Of *course* there's no way you'd know about modern design. And it's foolish of me to evaluate everything by current fads. Yes, Rissa—it *is* beautiful. Trust your own taste, dear. You won't go wrong."

Rissa laughed. "I'll have to learn a lot, won't I? But I have lots of time now. So let's sit down. Tell me about my parents."

They sat, but Camilla said, "Lots of time is what you *don't* have. Look, Rissa—you're on a short fuse. You have to get out, and fast. That's why I'm here."

"I don't understand. I trust you, but I don't understand."

"Now, look, girl—what do you think the State gets for its money, giving you umpty million Weltmarks?"

"I don't know. Oh, sure—I figured out that the one chance in a million helps keep the rest of the million quiet, but—"

"Figure a little further. You're good for about two months' free publicity to make everybody feel happy. Then what happens?"

"I don't know—how could I? What *does* happen?"

"The way it usually works—well, we have so many laws *nobody* can keep track—the Committee passes new ones all the time. And you're starting from scratch. So every now and then you'd break one."

"And they'd punish me? Fines? Jails?"

"They'd let them pile up until they had enough to look good in the records. Then—*without* publicity—they'd pick you up, declare your assets forfeit, and put you back in Welfare."

"No!" Rissa's hands clawed at her face; her body shook. Gently the older woman took her hands, then embraced her.

"It doesn't have to happen to *you*. There's a place to go— I've helped others—you'll be safe there. Now just listen a minute, will you?"

Still shuddering, Rissa nodded. She listened, and at the end of it she asked, "What about Ivan, my brother? And Uncle Voris?"

"There's not time to do it from here. The procedures would take too long—they'd stall, you see. And then they'd have you."

"But—to manage it from there? So *far?*"

"Not only safer, but easier. The Establishment where you're going—can pull strings I couldn't begin to reach."

"Very well." And then they talked of David Marchant and Selene Kerguelen.

Once Camilla said, "Do you know about your parents' deaths?"

"Uncle Voris told me, when I was first in Welfare. Colonel Osbert Newhausen. Every night, to remember, I repeat that name."

"He's a general these days. But you may as well forget him; you can't do anything."

"Then somewhere I will find someone who can."

RISSA'S net proceeds from the lottery came close to 23,000,000 Weltmarks; the gross, announced publicly, was 100,000,000. One Weltmark was roughly a day's wage for freepersons in unskilled labor; as a Welfare Client, Rissa had been "paid" a tenth of that—but had never had use of a centum of it. She had no way to gauge the magnitude of her new fortune; she only knew she was rich, legally adult and—for so long as she could manage it—free.

In Rissa's name, but by Camilla's instructions, the money

began to move toward Rissa's destination. She did not entirely understand the necessary ruses. "R. Kerguelen" invested in conglomerates with vast overseas holdings. A few days later the spelling changed to "R. Karguelen." Camilla laughed and said, "Even with the computer tech on our side, it cost a pretty bribe to throw UET's fund-flow monitors off the track."

"R. Karguelen's" assets, in short order, siphoned themselves southward—outside the jurisdiction of the Committee and of its masters, United Energy and Transport. Camilla said, "UET's safeguards, its controls, are so complex and interconnected that we can bollix one, and it sets the others against it, long enough to get you out."

And one evening Camilla came in and said, "You go tonight. Now's when you wear that wig. I have your tickets, and all—enough money for the trip. The passport's not as good as I'd like, but it should work."

Rissa looked at the picture. The wig was the same and the face could have been Rissa—or any one of a thousand others. The name was Antonia Duval; Rissa memorized it.

"Now here's the accounting," said Camilla. "Briefly, it's cost you a million, nearly—including my commission. Altruists have to live, too, you know. The rest is yours, and safe."

"I don't begrudge you, Camilla. Take more, if you wish."

"No need. I've got nearly enough now to do a bunk myself if I have to. But there's another job I must do first, anyway—and that one will put me over the top."

"As you say, then. Do I go soon? A copter again?"

"No—a groundcar this time—from the sub-basement, at the rear. In—let's see—about an hour." For a moment, silent and unsmiling, she looked at Rissa. "This is always the hard part—waiting to see if you make it. If you're caught, I'm dead or Welfared. And the driver—he's Underground, too. So be careful—Antonia."

"I will—oh, I will!"

When the time came, Rissa was prepared. The mirror and her passport showed a fair match. Camilla said, "Write to me—but not directly. At the Establishment they'll teach you the codings."

Rissa embraced her. "I'll write. And I'll never forget you."

F. M. Busby

● ● ●

THE sub-basement loomed in dimness; pillars divided her view. Near the rear entrance a light blinked; through the vast empty space she scuttled to a groundcar. Face unseen, the driver said, "Duval?"

"Yes."

"Get in." She did; the car crawled up a ramp and entered sparse street traffic. She did not know the destination and made no effort to orient herself, nor did she speak. At the airport the car stopped near the Air Latinas sign. The driver pointed.

"In there. And good luck . . . Duval. You know what to do."

"Thank you. Yes—I will not test the passport until you are away from here." He nodded; she got out, closed the door and entered the terminal. For ten minutes she stood, then approached the check-in counter. Under her breath she repeated Camilla's quick briefing.

SHE had no trouble; the passport worked. Her tickets, she found, put her aboard a low-level SST—not suborbital, due to an intermediate stop—in the Deluxe Tourist Coach section, Area B. Beyond, she saw Area A, and could find no distinction between the two. Shortly after takeoff, she slept.

The plane flew, landed, waited, took off, flew and landed again. At the terminal a man and woman met her. "Antonia Duval?"

"Yes." They waited, silent. She showed her passport.

The woman nodded. "All right. Come on." She followed them.

Once in the car and clear of the airport the man said, "So you made it. Welcome, Rissa Kerguelen. You're free now."

YOUNG RISSA

● ● ●

THE country was Argentina. The Establishment was a half-day's drive from Buenos Aires, and its proprietress was Erika Hulzein. At mid-morning, refreshed after sleeping in the car, bathed, and freshly clothed, Rissa met her.

Except for the white hair, worn loose around her face and cut at chin length, Madame Hulzein did not look her seventy years. Her body was trim; she moved smoothly. Seeing her face's youthful contours, Rissa deduced cosmetic surgery, but saw no telltale marks. Then she was caught by the gaze of deep-set blue eyes above the thin, hawklike nose, and the woman smiled.

"Yes, it takes money to hold your looks at my age. Luckily, I've got it. Now, then, girl—sit down and tell me your story. All of it; Camilla gave me only the outline. We have the rest of the morning; I've cleared my other appointments."

"But why—?"

"Because we have a lot of work to do, you and I—and I need to know exactly what we're starting with. So go ahead."

Rissa thought a moment, then began with her parents and early life. For a time she was afraid she was taking too long at it, but when she paused, Erika Hulzein smiled faintly and nodded for her to continue.

She came to that terrible day—her parents dead, the unfeeling Welfare agent—and found herself telling of her uncle giving her Selene. "But that's silly—a child's pretending—it's not important. What happened next was—"

"It is important—because it *was* important. Tell me . . ."

So Rissa forgot about time and described, as well as she could remember, all that had happened to her. She edited, of course, relating only the first or most memorable among similar events. She hardly noticed when a young woman brought a tray with coffee and thin slices of dark, pungent bread—but all the same, talking between bites, she ate and drank.

F. M. Busby

When she reached the point of her transfer to Postpube, and the surgery, Erika said, "Pause a moment. They said things you didn't understand? Can you remember *any* of it?"

"Uh—magnetic something—and the Underground making a stink. I—"

"And your uncle had entered a lawsuit! Ha!" Erika clapped her hands together. "You're not sterilized, girl—not permanently. Twenty to one, you're not!"

"But how—?"

"It's called a 'reversible.' Your Fallopian tubes—do you know what those are?" Rissa nodded. "Well, instead of tying them off in the usual way, a short length of each is replaced by plastic tubing, magnetically polarized. They're left sealed off, of course, but Welfare—the Committee—what the *scheiss*, it's all UET!—they have specially designed magnetic devices. Hold one of those against you at the proper spot, push the right buttons and turn the right dials—those magnetic sections open and close like faucets." She frowned. "They're hard to get, those machines—it's going to cost you—but with patience and bribery you'll control your own womb again!"

RISSA'S story continued. When it came to Gerard—the rape when she was near death, later the compulsory morning services—Erika shook her head. "So *that's* how Welfare teaches love. I imagine you don't care much for sex, do you?"

"No—except what I do by myself. Does any woman?"

Erika laughed, then sobered. "I don't mean to make fun of your misfortune. But—you'll learn, Rissa. Here, you'll learn! And now—go on with it."

"There's not much more." The lottery winning, the press interview, Camilla Altworth, and the escape. She laughed. "And is it my turn to ask?"

"What do you want to know?"

"Well—what happens now?"

Like gulls' wings, Erika's eyebrows lifted. "Camilla didn't tell you? Well, it's up to you, of course. You owe me nothing

—Camilla arranged your way this far. So you could take your money—the documents that give you control of it—and go to the city or elsewhere, and build your own life. You'd be safe enough. Whether I actually own this country is open to debate, but I have enough power to keep UET's hands out of it, and I do just that."

"But there is something more, isn't there? *What* didn't Camilla tell me?"

"What it is that I'm offering you. It doesn't come cheaply and it takes time—a million Weltmarks and at least a year." Erika raised a hand. "Let me finish. That million and that year buys you the best survival training package available on this planet. Here are some of the parts of it. . . ."

When Erika had finished, Rissa said, "If you—your Establishment—can teach me all that, the price seems cheap enough. Especially since it's quite obvious that if you wanted to, you could take all I have and leave me nothing."

"Ha! You're learning already. Shall we have lunch now?"

NEXT day it began. How it could all be done in one year, Rissa could not imagine. Mastery of several languages including variant speech patterns. Three distinct approaches to the art of political corruption. Proficiency at controlling vehicles on land or water, or in air—not in space, though, for Erika had no starship. *Yet*, Rissa reminded herself . . .

Polite conversation. Financial manipulation, including the legal aspects. More ways of armed and unarmed combat than she had known to exist. Psychology, with emphasis on the art of bluffing: when, with whom, and how much. Acting—not on stage but in life—and disguise. Drinking and doping without loss of aim, impetus, or clarity of intention. Sex in many fashions. And—she was eager to learn of this—ways to free her mind of old bondages.

The training began slowly, a little at a time. It grew in scope until she did not think her mind, her body, her time could hold it all. But somehow, she managed.

F. M. Busby

• • •

SHE also learned things outside her curriculum. She shared a room with Maria Faldane, a sultry swarthy girl a year older than Rissa, hailing from some part of Southwestern North America. Maria was several weeks ahead of Rissa in training —and a mine of gossip.

For instance: "Frieda Hulzein? She's thirty, so Erika was forty at the birth. Oh, parthenogenetic, of course, but gene-replicated—and fertile, with luck." At Rissa's inquiring look, Maria explained. "Gene-replicated means you get all your chromosomes, not just half like the oldtime haploid parthenoes. It's secret, how they do it—but what I heard, they get the nucleus of one ovum to fertilize another one. If you get the proper halves together, it works."

"And if you don't?"

"Then it's zerch—no result; try again." Then; "Have you seen much of Frieda?"

Rissa shook her head. "No—just now and then. She doesn't look as much like Erika as you'd expect, does she?" On Frieda, Erika's hawklike features were exaggerated—almost coarse, Rissa thought. And she moved less gracefully.

"Huh! Doesn't quite act like her, either. I tell you, Rissa, she scares me sometimes. You can't tell how she's likely to react. Does she scare you?"

Rissa thought. "No. In Welfare I never knew how the staff people would react. When I'm not sure, I don't say much; that's all."

"Yes." Maria nodded. "Well—*that* one doesn't have all her wheels on the ground, let me tell you."

The conversation shifted, and soon it was time for sleep. But next day Maria was absent from afternoon training. Long after dinner, moving slowly and stiffly, she entered their room. Rissa said, "What's the matter? What happened? Are you all right?"

Maria shook her head. "I don't want to talk any more about—about anything."

YOUNG RISSA

• • •

IN the realm of sex, Rissa learned that Gerard had known nothing of her body's ways—and very little, she suspected, about his own. Skilled men and women taught her how to give pleasure, and—equally important in some circumstances, perhaps—how to withhold it, to deny another's response. She discovered many enjoyments, but somehow—despite her new skills and those of her teachers—neither singly with another nor in varied groupings could she find the satisfaction she knew alone, late at night, in the way she had learned as a child. She knew that others had no such handicap but said nothing, feeling that the problem was hers to solve.

One day, resting, she lay beside two friends; even the incomplete fulfillment had been pleasant. She said, "Jorge—Cecily—am I progressing well in these things? How much more is there for me to learn?"

"Very little that's new to you," the woman said. "Wouldn't you agree, Jorge?"

"Yes. More practice, I think, on this and that. Oh, not this today. Rissa—in these matters you're superb. But on Tuesday—remember?"

"Yes. I was clumsy. And I forgot, until nearly too late, to—"

"Oh, never mind," said Cecily. "I don't think you'll forget again. Because I've noticed something—you never make the same mistake twice." She laughed. "You're doing fine, Rissa—maybe not as rapidly as in combat arts, but quite well."

Jorge said, "Another month, I'll bet on it, Rissa—you'll be up for your turn in Erika's private circle."

She shook her head. "Private circle?"

"Didn't your talkative roommate tell you? Erika keeps a rotating stable of concubines—both sexes—and she's not greedy about it. The system serves two purposes—it's also your final exams."

"I—" Rissa frowned. Remembering Maria's sudden turnabout, she said, "It may not be . . . wise . . . to discuss

F. M. Busby

Madame Hulzein's private life."

"Oh, Erika doesn't mind," said Cecily. "She makes no secret of it—and no apologies for *anything* she does."

"She doesn't have to," said Jorge. "Customs don't bind her."

Rissa said, "Nor laws, I understand."

"In this country, if a law annoys Erika, she has it changed."

"Somehow I don't think you're joking," said Rissa. "Or not by much." Slowly she rose, stretching. "I'm due for a session with Maestro Gomez. Today's task is to converse, ad lib and on cue, in the voice tones and speech patterns of two assumed identities he assigned me last week."

The others groaned. "I wish you luck," said Jorge. "That's something *I'm* not good at."

ON the day she could have died, Rissa learned a new thing about herself. She rode with Erika to the city, observed while the older woman visited branch offices; they lunched together. Ready to return, Erika said, "I'm a little tired; would you like to take us back?"

"Of course." Rissa liked aircars and handled them well. As Erika sat, relaxed, Rissa took the car up. "How about the shortcut, the gap through the foothills?" Eyes closed, Erika nodded.

Past the gap, emerging over a canyon, the motors failed. Abruptly the car dropped—boulders far below, the cliff looming—*We're dead!* Only seconds left . . .

But . . . it felt like *minutes*, as Rissa looked around her —rocks and trees, the cliff—a sloping ledge, and below that—

She steered at the ledge, grazed it broadside. Metal shrieked but did not crumple; the car was slowed. Next—*there*, the dropoff they had passed—where it curved and—

Back across the canyon, still plummeting, again she struck at a grazing slant—rebounded, hit again and skidded, metal screeching against rock—down the cliff as it curved to canyon floor. *Can this work? Why doesn't Erika—?*

Metal flew; windows sprang free of mountings. No steering now—she could not avoid the boulder, struck it glancing and now the car rolled, over and over. She felt nothing but roar of sound; then they stopped, and the roar was in her own ears.

"Erika!" The car sat tilted; she scrabbled free of her safety harness and clambered to see. "Are you all right?"

Blood streaked Erika's chin but she said, "Well enough—shaken, nicked a little, like yourself. My God! How did you do it? It seemed like hours."

Startled, Rissa said, "*Yes*—that's it! When I saw—we had no chance—it changed, like slow motion on Tri-V. I looked and looked a long time before I decided the ledge was best. Then—"

Wiping away blood, Erika smiled. "So you're another!" Rissa shook her head, waiting. "I call us adrenaline freaks—though that doesn't explain it. But when it's life or death, time *slows*—it did for me, too. When we get back—tomorrow, say —we'll test you."

The radio brought rescue. Next day, and following days, Erika tested Rissa against simulated emergencies—without success. "Well, some can train it; some can't. I can't, but hoped you could."

"Do you know why not?"

"Maybe we're too smart—can't fool ourselves about real danger. And I'm not risking you—*or* me—in a setup that could be fatal if the reaction isn't enough to handle it.

"But you can keep in mind, Rissa—when it comes down to cases, you've got an ace in the hole!"

RISSA'S skills grew, and with them her self-assurance. She had her turn—not quite as soon as Jorge had predicted—with Erika's "stable"—and was surprised by the real warmth and intimacy within that changing group. When the turn ended, Erika talked with her, the two alone. "You're a love, girl— we're all agreed on that. Now this problem of yours—oh, it's

obvious, to me, at least, that you have to fake the high points
—well, I think you'll overcome it sooner or later. The odds are
good. And for most purposes you do fake it well. But—and
this is vital—don't *ever* do so with anyone who is truly, personally important to you. Do you understand why?''

''Because if I fool someone, there's no way for that person
to know I still need help?''

''That's part of it. Where one fails, two may succeed—but
only if both know something's needed. But also, you can't
help feeling contemptuous of anyone you can lie to, suc-
cessfully. And contempt is a very nasty poison.''

''I see. And I'm sorry, Erika, because you and others here
are important to me.''

The older woman shook her head. ''Not the way I meant.
You're here for the year, and then you'll be gone. I spoke of
the kind of importance that sometimes has a future to it.''

She gripped Rissa's shoulder and shook it gently. ''Now you
must get on with other matters. I'll have your things moved to
your old room; you have it to yourself now—the Faldane girl's
working at our city offices.'' She paused. ''By the way—have
you had any luck, finding your uncle?''

Rissa shook her head and left.

COMPUTER tapes can be erased; Rissa found no hint that Voris
Kerguelen had ever existed. She had better luck with Ivan; he
had been moved, but she discovered his new location. When
she was certain, she went to Madame Hulzein.

''I've found my brother.''

''Well, get him out. I've taught you how, haven't I?''

''Yes. To begin with, my money—or yours, for that matter
—is useless in North America if recognized as such; it would
be confiscated.'' She awaited Erika's nod. ''So we work
through established drops and code all communications.''

''Go ahead.''

''I will. But, your advice—which drop should I use?
Camilla?''

"No. She wound up her work a few days ago and skipped to Australia two jumps ahead of a Committee arrest order. She sends her best wishes, by the way—says she'll answer your latest message when she gets settled and has time."

Rissa smiled. "I am glad. But then, who. . . ?"

"Let me think. Do you know the New Mafia codes and dropsigns?"

"I've seen them—I know where to look. But—can that group be trusted?"

Erika grinned. "They play a double game—always. But I'm one they don't cross."

"Then may I use your sign group in the message?"

"Not the personal one; use the one that says you speak *for* me. It's clear enough in the readout."

"All right. And thank you, Erika."

IN due time, Ivan Marchant arrived. They did not recognize one another.

"Ivan? Is it you? I'm Rissa."

The man's thin face twitched. "I uphold the principle of total Welfare."

"Ivan!" She turned to Erika. "Are you sure this is my brother?"

"The records say so. Fingerprints and retinal patterns match."

Rissa went to him. "It *is* you, Ivan—isn't it?"

"Ivan Marchant defends the ethics of Total Welfare and always will!"

Erika Hulzein embraced them both. "I'll take him, Rissa, and try to grow back his mind—what they've left of it. I can't promise full recovery, but I'll try. My fee's only half of what it was for you, because he can't use more than half the training, probably." Rissa hugged her brother once more; then an attendant led him away. Erika said, "Don't give up yet, on him; there's still a chance."

Rissa spat. "There's a *chance* that UET's Presiding Committee will grow wings. They've canceled all future elections; it's the next logical step. But I won't sit quietly in a duck blind, waiting for them to fly over!''

Erika's eyes narrowed. "I thought you'd dropped that idea."

Half smiling, half snarling, Rissa answered. "Oh, I have—I can't afford it." Political assassinations, she had found, came high; all her wealth would barely have bought the death of any one Committee member. "It's more important that I get off Earth."

She did not mention her independent negotiations with the New Mafia. The Committee was out of her reach, but she had not forgotten Osbert Newhausen—and she felt her plans for that man might shock even Erika Hulzein. Not death—for David and Selene, for Rissa's eleven years in Welfare and Ivan's damaged mind, death was not sufficient. She hoped the general would live at least eleven years. . . .

To Erika, though, she said only, "You've taught me a great deal. But one thing I knew already—settle for what you can get."

"Not too cheaply, however. Remember, Rissa—sometimes you can get more than you might think."

Rissa laughed. "Yes, I know. And with your training to help me, perhaps I will."

HER million-Weltmark year neared its end; looking back from what she was to what she had been, Rissa felt that it was worth every centum she had paid.

Now, readying herself to leave, she conferred more often with Erika. During one such meeting, Frieda Hulzein entered. The brown hair of Erika's heiress was only beginning to show gray, but in some ways the mother seemed the younger.

Frieda sat. "Rissa Kerguelen, isn't it?" Rissa nodded. "Considering the time you've been here, we haven't seen much of each other. I almost feel you've been avoiding me."

Rissa said, "Your responsibilities and my training didn't

overlap greatly. You are, of course, primarily concerned with management and administration. Your subordinates had charge of my studies in those areas."

"I suppose so. Well, now—I understand you're leaving us soon? And like all youngsters, ready to go out and take on the whole world?"

"No. Quite the opposite. I'm ready, as soon as possible, to take *off* this world."

Erika said, "So you'll be in touch, you two, over the years. Frieda—we'll be handling Rissa's Earthside affairs—you've seen the agreements, or will. All standard, with the code-changing sequences staggered on the ABC contingency patterns."

Frieda nodded. "That's sound." She looked at Rissa. "Are you sure you understand how those progressions work? Over the light-years, they can get complicated."

"I think so," Rissa said. "As an example, if the mutual lag is fifteen years and my chart begins with AB7, then my first message upon landing would start with—"

She continued the explanation through the first two changes; then Frieda waved a hand. "All right; you'll manage." She stood. "I'm expecting a call. Another time, then."

When she had left, Erika said, "You don't like Frieda, do you?"

"It's as I said—we've never had cause to become acquainted."

"She's a little hard to know, I realize. But are you sure that's all?"

"What more could there be?"

Erika frowned, but only briefly. "Quite a lot. And if you were staying here much longer I'd find out, too. You're a good bluffer but I taught your teachers. Well, it's not important—over umpteen light-years, personalities don't matter much."

"No." And Rissa left to see to her preparations.

* * *

WAITING while certain financial arrangements were completed, she overstayed her year by three weeks. Her investments had prospered; her net worth after all expenses—including the Newhausen contract—was well over 25,000,000 Weltmarks. Part of her wealth she would take off Earth; the rest would work for her in several countries, each group of assets held jointly in the names of two or more manufactured identities. Sometimes, though not usually, her own name also appeared. The network was arranged so that she could reach any holding from any identity in not more than two stages.

Nonexistent *personae*, she had found, cost money and required supporting paraphernalia. She had three—Lysse Harnain, Tari Obrigo, and Cele Metrokin—and none of them, in speech or appearance, would be mistaken for any other or for herself.

Except for three items, she had stayed clear of North America. Theft and delivery of the fertility-control device was as expensive as Erika had warned, but finally the thing arrived. There was, of course, the Newhausen contract. And Lysse Harnain, Tari Obrigo, and Cele Metrokin, between them and jointly, held nearly 4,000,000 Weltmarks in UET voting stock. That holding was Rissa's leverage to get her off Earth.

So it was Lysse Harnain, aged twenty-eight, attractive but not pretty, who said good-bye to Erika. Lysse spoke in a shrill little-girl voice. Plastic inserts widened her nostrils; a removable cap gave her a crooked front tooth. Her hair, temporarily reddened, she wore in tight curls pulled to the crown of her head. Thin, indetectable plastic lenses changed her gray eyes to green and would mislead any retinal-pattern check. Tissue-thin appliqués on her fingertips carried the fabricated print patterns on file for Lysse Harnain. Duplicates of these accessories, and their counterparts for Tari Obrigo and Cele Metrokin, were well hidden in her handbag and luggage. The magnetic "faucet handle" masqueraded as part of her hair dryer. Thus equipped, she reported to Erika.

The older woman reached to take both her hands, looked closely at her and nodded. "You'll do," she said. "Now—sit down—I'm glad I got back from the city before you left. Are your plans still the same?"

"Almost. I'm not risking North America at all; UET's subsidiary in Japan seems a safer bet. About a month from now a ship leaves Hokkaido base for Terranova by way of Far Corner. I'll book all the way through, of course, but—"

"I thought the Twin Worlds was your goal."

"My transfer point, you mean? Yes—it was. But your latest Intelligence report—it came while you were gone—says UET smells Escaped Ship activity there. By the time I arrived, those planets might be buttoned up tight."

"And so?"

"The report also mentions—and this part is from the Underground—Escaped Ships' contact at Far Corner. And my goal is wherever those ships make their base—the Hidden Worlds."

"If the Hidden Worlds exist . . ."

"You know they do! They *must!*"

Erika chuckled. "Of course. Forgive an old woman's jealousy. For me, at my age, they do not." Then, "Far Corner, eh? I have an agent there—an Asian—former space pilot. He lost an arm and they left him at the first stop."

Rissa nodded. "Osallin, you mean. I've seen his dossier. He has no love for UET."

"Does anyone? I doubt those *scheisskopfs* love themselves! Now, then—you'll send word?"

"Of course I will, when I can. And you—?"

The old woman shook her head. "By the time your first message could arrive, I'm not likely to be here. But Frieda will do as I would."

Though Rissa was not as certain of Frieda as Erika was, she nodded and said, "Yes. Of course."

"Well, then—do you want to see your brother before you go?"

"No." Erika's psych-techs had freed Ivan from much of UET's implanted compulsion, but his intelligence had only begun to recover, and slowly. "I know he's safe here—but just in case, it's as well that only you know me in this guise."

"Of course." Both women stood. Erika pulled the girl close and gave her cheek a dry kiss. "All right, Rissa—Lysse—I wish you didn't have to say good-bye in that whiny little voice, though I'm gratified that you maintain characterization so well." She sighed. "Anyway—you're as capable as *I* can manage, and more so than most I've trained. I hope you get—well, whatever it is you want. You've earned it."

Rissa looked at the woman she had known only a year; the woman who had changed her from an ignorant child to an able, competent person skilled in ways that a year ago she could not have imagined—the woman she could never see again. She blinked away tears; the kiss she gave was neither dry nor perfunctory.

"Earned it? Not yet, Erika—but I intend to."

When she turned away, she did not look back.

A DIRIGIBLE steamer took her to Mexico City, a suborbital SST to Tokyo Complex, and a hydrofoil to UET's Hokkaido spaceport. She knew the hotels there, under whatever names, were UET-owned and subject to electronic surveillance; she took care not to breach her Lysse Harnain identity. Using stockholder's privilege, she booked passage on the *MacNamara* at company discount, bypassing the usual waiting list and screening process. She stayed in her suite and dined from the automated room-service.

Newsfax was part of the service; she made a show of scanning everything concerning the Western Hemisphere and Europe, but paid heed only to the North American printouts, with special attention to that continent's Midwest area.

A week before her scheduled departure she found the item she wanted. General Osbert Newhausen's wives and co-husbands had filed unanimously to divorce him, and the general was hospitalized following a suicide attempt. Rissa gave no outward sign of her intense satisfaction. The New Mafia representative had told the truth; the mutated virus was effective, as described.

Although she pretended—for the sake of possible observers—to continue to read the printouts, she had no further interest in Earth's affairs. During her last evening, however, she used the suite's communicator keyboard to dispatch a coded note to Erika Hulzein via a Buenos Aires message drop. Decoded, it would read, "On my way tonight. Greatest thanks for all you have done, and love to poor Ivan."

IT may have been the note that was almost her undoing. Leaving from the lower-level terminal, she timed her movements so as to be alone in the tube-capsule that would take her to the ship. But at the last moment a bulky woman ran to reopen the closing door and crowded in to join her. The woman wore the red and blue plastic hood-mask of the North American Committee Police; behind it showed only shadowed lips and eyes. Rissa looked at her and said nothing, thinking, *it could be coincidence—but it smells wrong!*

"Going off Earth?" The voice was deep, and unexpectedly soft.

All right—the policebitch would have seen the records; there was no point in lying. "Yes, to Terranova. And you?"

A laugh, not soft like the voice, but harsh. "No such luck. Just a little business at the port. Where do you come from?"

She'd know that, too. Lysse Harnain could be—no doubt *had* been—traced back to South America. Yet it had not been feasible to change identities at the brief stops. "Most recently, Argentina."

"Where in that country?"

The Committee's hound knew, all right—but make *her* say it. "A small town, near Buenos Aires. You wouldn't have heard of it."

"But I've heard of it many times—including just this evening. It's rather notorious."

"Then why do you ask?"

The heavy shoulders shrugged. "One way to get to the real questions." Rissa did not answer. The woman said, "We know you come from Hulzeins'."

A moment for thought. "I did visit a person of that name. What does that—or this place, for that matter—have to do with *your* jurisdiction?"

"At Hulzeins', is there a girl named Rissa Kerguelen?"

By God, they never quit looking! "There are many girls."

"About seventeen—slim—dark hair. Did you see her?"

"I don't believe I met her. Why?"

"Wanted on a Committee warrant. The charge is treason. Hulzein should know better than to harbor such persons."

Rissa manufactured a laugh. "I doubt that Madame Hulzein's much concerned with your Committee's machinations. But, yes—now I remember—this girl you mention—she must be the one who killed herself when she saw her brother again. A childish thing to do, but she was barely of legal age. Erika was quite disappointed in her."

"You're sure?" The woman's grip hurt Rissa's shoulder; she was tempted to break a finger of the offending hand, but waited.

"You're hurting me! No, of course I'm not sure. I heard a lot of stories—who's to say which were true? I didn't follow the gossip closely, anyway. I had my own concerns."

The hand gripped harder. "I'm sure you did—Rissa."

It was time to act. Past time—the port was near. Maybe the sniffing bitch was only guessing, but the chance wasn't worth it. She felt the jolt of peril—now, as in the aircar, time *slowed*. She turned to face the plastic mask, took a breath, and drove the heel of her hand as hard as she could, up to the hidden nose. With luck she could have driven bone splinters into the brain, but the plastic was too rigid; her blow slipped off its bulge. The woman half-screamed—in fear, or was it anger?—and thrust out a meaty hand to squeeze Rissa's throat. Behind the mask her eyes shone, almost like burning coals. Rissa pointed stiff fingers at those eyes and jabbed.

She did not know how well or ill she wrought; the woman cried out and clapped her hands to her face. Rissa reached across her; overriding the safety interlock she button-punched the door open. She raked a heel down the woman's shin and drew a yelp of pain; then she braced herself and *pushed*, until the woman's head and shoulders were outside, rubbing against

the tube wall as the capsule sped. The policewoman screamed
—then friction took hold and the capsule swayed with the im-
pact. Rissa heard bones snap as the woman's body was pulled
outside to be crushed in the narrow space and vanish behind.
Almost, Rissa followed it—she barely managed to disengage
and catch herself against the door frame.

She punched the door closed again and sat back, panting,
fighting for calm. A pang wrenched her—she had never killed
before. Yet what choice had she?

A minute or so later, the capsule came to a halt. She left it
and walked out of the terminal, across the spaceport to the
ship.

UET's stockholders had first option on the freeze-chambers.
Rissa had considered the matter. Overall time dilation for the
trip—not the one she had booked, but the shorter one she intended—was slightly less than eighteen. Twelve years for the
price of, perhaps, eight months. Faster ships made better
tradeoffs, but none were scheduled to meet her need. The
question was, did she want to spend those eight months awake
on a cramped ship, all the while alert to keep the role of Lysse
Harnain? Not really, she decided. And the freezing and revival
procedures, Erika had assured her, posed no threat to her disguise.

So she "bumped" a man who could have bought and sold
her ten times over—but who owned less UET stock—and prepared to enter freeze. To justify being revivified at the stop-
over, she mentioned an investment possibility at Far Corner.
Then she went to chilly sleep.

When the ship landed and she was awakened and treated,
she went aground with only her essential luggage, content to
let the rest go on to a destination that was not hers. So far, she
felt, she was well ahead of the game. It remained to be seen
what turns that game would take in future.

•   •   •

SHE did not risk UET's spaceport hostelry; near the ship she hailed a groundcab, and once inside, took certain precautions with her appearance. The cab took her to and past the town of Second Site, to a ramshackle inn called the First Ever. It catered largely, the driver told her, to miners and trappers.

Inside, signing the register as Tari Obrigo, she paid triple the usual rate because she needed a room to herself. The landlord looked at her—head covered by a hood, her face veiled—and grinned behind his grizzled beard.

"Private doings—eh, Ms. Obrigo?"

"I am accustomed to privacy and willing to pay for it." Her voice was soft, slightly accented, and she spoke in the precise manner of Tari Obrigo.

"No offense, Ms. Here—I'll show you your room. Want any help with your duffel?"

"No—well, yes—you might take this one. It is not heavy, but with the other two, awkward to carry." The man nodded and led her to a second-floor room, complete with bathing and toilet facilities. Going to the room's one window, he opened the curtains.

"Nice view across town," he said. "Spaceport just past the valley, and the big trees behind it." He made no move to leave.

"Yes—thank you." Far Corner custom, she recalled, added all tips to the final billing, so that wasn't what he was waiting for. "I think that is all, for the moment."

"You haven't said—you want to take your meals here, or out?"

Annoyed, she shook her head. "Can I not do either, as is convenient?"

"Sure. Cost you more, though. Cheaper to sign up for meals with the room."

"I cannot help that. My plans are . . . flexible."

"Suit yourself, Ms. Well—anything you need, just ask."

"Yes. I will. Thank you," and finally the man left. She locked the door, reclosed the curtains and removed her veil and hooded cloak.

The next hour she spent transforming Lysse Harnain to Tari

Obrigo—age twenty-two—dark brown eyes, black hair falling in loose curls around her face and brushing her shoulders. Her nose was Rissa's own, but with a small fleshy mole alongside the left nostril. The crooked tooth-cap was replaced by one that gave prominence to the upper front incisors. Tweezers emphasized the arching of her brows. And she did not forget to change her fingerprints.

The mirror satisfied her. Now she was ready to show her face—Tari Obrigo's—on Far Corner.

OSALLIN'S office, she knew, was in the Independent Brokers' warehouse; she had seen the looming structure from the groundcab. She guessed its distance at roughly three kilometers and decided to walk. Stepping out into cool early-afternoon sunlight, she enjoyed the use of her muscles in Far Corner's gravity, nearly a fourth slighter than Earth's. She faced a breeze; from the forest beyond the spaceport she smelled strange, pleasant fragrances.

She approached the building from the warehouse side and walked another two hundred meters to reach the office section. Entering, she came into a lobby that contained several receptionists' desks—three occupied and one occupant not busy. Rissa approached; the thin, elderly woman looked up.

"I would like to meet with Broker Osallin."

The woman cleared her throat. "I must approve all the Broker's appointments. Your name?"

Rissa smiled. "If you would inform him, please, that I bring greeting from Erika?"

The other paused, then nodded. "Oh, yes—certainly." She spoke into a hushtalk handset, then said, "It will be only a few minutes, Ms. Be seated, if you like."

"Thank you." But Rissa had no desire to sit; she strolled around the lobby, looking at pictures and at glass-enclosed exhibits of Far Corner's produce. After perhaps ten minutes, the woman called to her and gave directions to Osallin's office, two floors above. Again, she decided to walk.

F. M. Busby

•   •   •

THE office was small, cluttered, and brightly lit. The man was short and wide, with a face to match. When he smiled she saw three gold teeth and a space where a bicuspid was missing. He held out his single hand, the left. "Erika sent you? From Earth?"

She found the handshake awkward. He released her hand and motioned for her to sit, facing him across the desk. "Not exactly," she said. "Erika was my mentor and my friend. She is not my employer; I have none."

Osallin pushed graying hair back from his forehead. "This is a social call, not business? And I don't know your name yet, do I?"

"It is business, also. I am going farther out. Erika suggested that she—her Establishment—and I, work through you as our relay point, for financial and other communications."

"All right—fine. On all transactions I charge five percent of gross. Other communications, courtesy of the house. You still haven't said who you are, though."

"Establishment secrecy applies. Agreed?" The man nodded. "I am here as Tari Obrigo. Other names that may apply in our dealings together and with Erika's group are Lysse Harnain, Cele Metrokin, and Rissa Kerguelen."

Abruptly, he sat straight. "You're *that* one!"

"I do not understand. You have heard something? How?"

"You landed today with the *MacNamara*; right? Well, there's faster ships. One that left Earth not long after you did, arrived here—oh, call it two months ago. With a packet for you from Erika, for one thing. And, for another, a UET agent.

"You can forget two of those names. Harnain's red-tabbed here and on Terranova—by the time you could get there, I mean—at the least. As well as on Earth. Mostly on suspicion, Erika thinks, but still—there it is. The other, though—Kerguelen—I'm forgetting I ever heard that one, and I suggest you do the same."

Her hand made a sidewise, brushing motion. "Yes—perhaps—probably. But what about the UET agent? No one followed me today."

"You were booked through to Terranova; he went on to there. I checked around, as Erika's letter requested, and I'm pretty sure he hired some local talent to watch for you when the *MacNamara* showed up. Would he have a picture of you to give them?"

"I should not think so. Only a description, if that."

Osallin's fingers worried his left earlobe. "After you got off the ship, how long were you visible as Harnain?"

"Hardly at all. I came aground wearing a cape with the hood up, and obtained a groundcab almost immediately. Once inside it I donned a veil; before that, I coughed occasionally to give me the excuse to hold a handkerchief to my nose and mouth. The driver would not recognize me—and the next time anyone saw my face, it was this one."

"Hmm." The man's fingers drummed on the desk. "If UET's locals don't have boarding clearance, likely they didn't spot you. If they do, they're employees and can't get off-port until their shifts end. Either way, they can't connect Harnain with Obrigo. Except . . ."

"Through the driver?" She shook her head. "That one was too busy arguing with some functionary about where it was permitted to park and to pick up passengers. She did not look at me—more than a brief glance—until I was veiled."

"But if an employee paid by UET saw you and saw the driver? Your clothing—"

Rissa laughed. "Osallin, there is no such thing as assured immunity. But Erika taught me to gauge odds, and here I adjudge them good. Only one thing perturbs me—*why* should UET go to so much trouble regarding the person whose name we have agreed to forget? Not the money, surely—to UET, that must be a trifle."

Osallin scowled. "Erika didn't give you enough background. Perhaps even *she* doesn't realize how rigid the UET's policies are."

"And neither do I. Will you tell me?"

"It's simple—they *won't* lose face. You got fame when you

won the lottery, and notoriety when you escaped North America—now you're an Underground hero until they catch you. They don't like that."

"No." Rissa managed a shaky laugh. "I suppose they don't. But out *here*—so far away, so many years?"

"If you're caught, they profit. A trifle, you say? Perhaps not so trifling, with Erika handling your affairs over the course of years. But that money on Earth is untouchable until you're in custody or proved dead. Then, with a little routine chicanery, it's UET's." He waved away her protest. "And don't forget—you paid your way but their agents ride free, except for the wasted years of their lifetimes. To UET, the cost of pursuit is trivial."

She shuddered. "They are not human, are they?"

"Of course they are." His tone was cheerful. "Wherever did you get the idea that 'human' is a synonym for 'good'?" She could find no answer.

"Well, then, Tari Obrigo, it's time you looked at what Erika sent you." She leafed through the papers; all was as she and Madame Hulzein had agreed. One-half the profits of Rissa's investments, after commission, forwarded to—and later through—Osallin's agency. Any net loss over a given period would be carried against future gains, but this initial profit voucher was over 1,000,000 Weltmarks. She calculated five percent and wrote a draft to Osallin's credit before inspecting the other material.

She sensed that the man was looking at her and raised her head to return his gaze. He said, "Are Erika's reports satisfactory?"

"Oh, yes." She paused, frowning. "Need I tell you that I trust Erika—and by her word, you also?"

Osallin exhaled a deep breath. "Hah!" Gently his closed fist thumped the desk. "That's what I wanted to hear. Now, then—what comes next? Where do you go? Or do I need to know that?"

She nodded, swinging the dark curls. "Of course you do, if we are to work together. But where? I do not yet know."

"You don't? I would have thought—"

"Where do the Escaped Ships go? The Hidden Worlds . . ."

Silently he looked at her, then said, "So that's it. I should have known."

"I do not understand you. Where *else* would I wish to go?"

His hand kneaded the stump at his right shoulder. "She's been wanting a look-in there—I knew that, of course—and why not? And so here you are."

"Erika? She will not be *alive*, Osallin, when I get . . . there, wherever. Or at least, not when word from me could reach Earth. This is entirely my idea, not Erika's."

"The Hulzeins aren't too proud to use others' ideas. And of all people, they're specially equipped to take the long view."

Rissa pondered his words. "What do you mean?"

His eyes narrowed. "Do you know who Erika *is*—and Frieda? Do you know about the others?"

"What others? What has anyone else to do with it?"

"Erika's mother, Renalle. And Heidele, her grandmother."

She shook her head. "No. She said nothing of them. Why—?"

"The Hulzein Establishment," he said. "Founded by Heidele, inherited by Renalle and then Erika, with Frieda next in line. And what has Frieda named her daughter?"

"I did not know she had one. Does she? And how can you know it would be a daughter?"

"She'll have one by now, if she can. And the Hulzeins have no sons—parthenogenesis doesn't work that way."

She gasped. "Of course. I know about Erika and Frieda, yes. But—how many?"

His chuckle conveyed no humor. "Frieda's daughter would be the fifth of the line. That's why I'm worried."

"Again, Osallin, I do not understand you."

"The copy-machine effect," he said. "What happens when you make a copy of a copy of a copy? You lose the fine detail; that's what. And when it's genetic endowment you're dealing with . . ."

He shrugged. "It wasn't a problem with the one-parent children late in the previous century, the fad that sprang up among the extreme elements of Female Liberation. Those offspring were—haploid, I think the term is—and infertile."

"I have heard of the movement, but very little about it."

"It died under UET, with all the rest of freedom." He scratched his nose. "Anyway, I'm not sure whether it was Heidele herself or someone else who developed the gene-replication system of parthenogenesis, to produce fertile offspring. But I know the rest of the history pretty well.

"The method never worked perfectly, but Heidele was lucky; she got Renalle on the first try, I hear. Renalle had two miscarriages and one monster—destroyed, of course—before Erika. And Erika—I don't know the details but it took her fifteen years to produce Frieda—with some serious congenital defects."

"I—I did not know . . ."

"Well, you wouldn't—they were correctible, mostly. But my point is, if Frieda doesn't introduce outside genes—have herself a two-parent child—the Hulzein line may end with her. And then what happens to the Establishment? How do we trust someone we've never met, who's *not* essentially our friend Erika, or even personally selected by her?"

The idea was new; she considered it. Time and space; yes. "We will have to. Just as I will someday have to trust—whoever succeeds you here, if I travel between worlds to any extent."

He grinned. "True. Except that I'm relying on my judgment, not my genes, when it's time to choose that successor."

Slowly, she nodded. "Yes, I see the difference. But you have a reason for telling me all this. What is it?"

"I suggest that you transfer more of your assets out of Hulzein hands and Hulzein knowledge. And build yourself at least one identity that's not in Erika's records. Just in case. That's what I'm doing." Once more he grinned. "And if you think a convincing, operative prosthetic arm isn't costing me a packet—think again!"

She frowned, they slowly nodded. "Yes, of course. Erika would approve, if she allowed herself to see the problem."

"Maybe she does see it. I'm merely providing against the chance that she doesn't."

"Yes." She thought. "Perhaps, Osallin, you can help me with the new identity before I leave here?"

"Certainly. You have a name in mind, and other details?"

She considered. "Laura Konig—blue eyes, light brown hair, native to this planet or brought here as an infant. Other details as you choose. All right?"

"Good enough. And I don't keep detailed records of such matters. Only the names—no cross-references, except in my head."

"Good. It is settled then. Now—can you get me contact with an Escaped Ship? And if so, how soon?"

"Hmmm—you missed one here, by about a week. The next—"

"Last week? No—I saw the board at the port. The only recent departure was UET's *J.E. Hoover.*"

Osallin laughed. "*Our* part of Far Corner knows, so no harm in telling you. The *Hoover*—if it were known to be Escaped it wouldn't appear on the port's docket. But Bernardez, the new captain—he's smart enough to forward faked reports to Earth. Quite handy—until UET eventually catches on—for an Escaped Ship to keep its pipeline open to information and Weltmarks."

"Then Escape is on a larger scale than Earth realizes?"

"Considerably. Erika—the Hulzeins—will know about the *Hoover* when they get my next dispatches. But with luck the Committee may be fooled for a long time yet." He opened a drawer and brought out a bottle and two glasses. "Let's drink to luck!"

The amber liquid was clear and sparkling; they touched glasses and she sipped. "This is new to me. It is quite tart; I like it. Is it a local product?"

"From the forest yonder; the berry grows on a parasitic vine. Funny thing—in the raw state it's deadly poison and *smells* like it. Heat of distillation breaks up the alkaloid molecule."

"You know a lot about Far Corner, Osallin."

"That's my business. Part of it, anyway."

"Yes. Now—about other Escaped Ships. Do you know—?"

He shook his head. "Nothing definite; only rumor. It could be two weeks, or six months—depending on what kind of planet you want to go to."

"Kind? What kinds are there? And where?"

"I don't know where. Ships don't give out that information—you can see why. The Hidden Worlds have names or numbers, and the ships will tell you about climates and populations—things like that, so you won't end up on a swamp planet if you prefer deserts. But actual locations are secret. What you and I don't know, we can't let slip to the wrong parties."

"Of course. But you can put me in touch?"

"And recommend you." He looked at his watch. "My next appointment's overdue. Oh, it's all right, Tari—it won't hurt for them to simmer a little before they hear my offer. But I judge that the time's about right. So if you'll excuse me? I've enjoyed talking with you. Oh, yes—you're staying where?"

She stood. "At the First Ever, near the edge of town."

"Good. But it isn't, you know—the first, I mean. The third built here, maybe. But the others are gone now—burned or torn down. So I don't blame old Charling for boosting his place a bit."

She extended her own left hand, so the handshake was less awkward. "When shall I—?"

"I'll send word; wait for it. Meanwhile—get out and see the country, why don't you? The worlds are so far apart—it's a shame to be on one and waste it."

"That is a good suggestion. Thank you, Osallin." Rissa turned and left. In the lobby a man and woman argued. She waited a moment. The receptionist called a name; the two rose, still bickering, and went to the staircase. She resisted the urge to smile; the wait had softened them up for Osallin, well enough.

IN the chilly twilight of Far Corner's short day she walked back to the First Ever. The landlord greeted her. "Have a good stroll, Ms. Obrigo?"

"Quite enjoyable, Mr. Charling . . . you *are* Mr. Charling?"

"Well, well—somebody tipped my ident, eh?"

"I mentioned the inn; someone told me the owner's name."

"Well and good; it's no secret. Now—can I help you?"

"Yes. I would like to take dinner here this evening."

"Sure. Dining room's around the corner there," and he motioned. "Dinner's served over two hours; you're about smack in the middle of it, right now. Sign by the door tells the mealtimes." She nodded, and he said, "Hey—you got a Far Corners watch?"

"No, I am afraid not."

"Rent you one, long as you want, while you're here. Tenth of a Weltmark per day—rental applies on buying if you decide to stay." She initialed the agreement on her account card and took the watch, then visited her room briefly and went to dinner. Tired, for it was still her first day out of freeze, she ate a light meal—native meats and vegetables with pleasant but unremarkable flavors. Back in her room she postponed thought and retired early.

FOLLOWING Osallin's advice, Rissa spent her next days exploring the countryside within reach of Second Site—on foot, by groundcar, and by air-flitter. She stalked gently through forest and once saw a rare swarming of the furry hive-flyers. For three days she trekked across the High Desert and inspected ruins left by an unknown species that built its doorways approximately one meter high and two wide. A tugboat, towing an ore barge, carried her half the length of the New Amazon river. She rode a flitter to the Heavy Sea and walked its beaches, inhaling the rich, pleasant aroma of the organic —and possibly living—body of liquid.

Returning a day later to the First Ever, she found a message from Osallin. "Come immediately. I have two prospects."

ACROSS his desk Osallin handed her a package. "First, here's your new identity kit—Laura Konig, per specifications. The eye-stickums are a darker blue than I expected, but on such short notice I had to take what was available."

"I am sure they will be all right. What is the cost?"

He waved his hand. "Hardly a nibble off my commission on your shipment from Erika. No charge—just part of the service."

"I thank you, Osallin."

"Anytime, Tari. Now, then—two Escaped Ships are in. Or rather, one's down and the other lands tomorrow. The question is, which do you want?"

She laughed. "How could I know, until you tell me of them?"

"The one at the port is called—renamed—*Ridgerunner*; it's one of the first to Escape. Good ship, good captain. Freeze-chambers in top shape. But its next two stops are at pioneer worlds, sparsely populated. I doubt that's what you have in mind."

"And the other?"

"Its destination's ideal—Number One, the first and most developed Hidden World. The colony got a big lift some years back when a ship Escaped with a cargo of frozen sperm and ova—and the artificial wombs to gestate them—intended to grow cheap labor for UET's mines on Iron Hat. I guess it was rough for a while—the first settlers raising kids at a ratio of maybe fifty children to one adult—but they made it." He looked down at his hand, then up again. "And—I don't know much about it, but there's a Hulzein connection on the planet."

Rissa waited but he said no more. "I gather, Osallin, that something about this choice is less than ideal?"

"The ship—*Inconnu* it's called, these days. Even among the Escaped—who all raid UET colonies when they can, of course—it's considered a bit of an outlaw. It's the only armed ship ever taken, and the captain—Tregare, his name is—took command by mutiny *after* Escape. Some say he takes on supplies and forgets—at gunpoint—to pay for them. And it's known that at Freedom's Ring he dispossessed the crew of another Escaped Ship and put his own cadre aboard. A lot of people think he's trying to build a fleet—maybe take over *all* the Escaped Ships."

She shook her head. "He cannot do it. Not in one man's lifetime. The logistics of star travel are against him."

"Maybe. But the question is—do you want to ride with a man like that?"

Rissa stretched, leaned back and ran both hands through her hair. "A moment, Osallin. Hmmm—I will need a lock box, about this big—" She gestured. "—with a photolock keyed to my—to Rissa Kerguelen's retinal patterns. Can you provide one and code it?"

"I can have it done, sure. But—"

"Are there rumors of harm to Tregare's passengers? Deaths or disappearances? Complaints?"

"Not that I know of."

"Then tomorrow, or whenever he is not busy, let us go and talk with Tregare."

Smiling, Osallin slapped his hand on the desk. "Somehow I knew you were going to say that!"

TREGARE'S first day aground, he would not see them. Nor the second. On the third day, Osallin took Rissa aboard *Inconnu*.

The two were shown to the captain's quarters. Tregare—a tall, sallow man with curly black hair over a high forehead —did not impress Rissa greatly. His bony face bore a milder expression than she had expected. His left cheek carried the tattoo that denoted rank in UET's space fleet; looking closely, Rissa saw that part of the pigments did not match, that his rank at Escape had been Third Officer. The rest of the tattoo, upgrading him to captain, had been added later and less expertly.

Without preamble the man said, "Passage to Number One. I have room for one, only."

"I wish passage; my friend Osallin does not. How much?"

Tregare grinned. After a few seconds he said, "What am I bid?"

"Bid?"

"I'm not running a charity, Ms. Obrigo. Highest bidder rides."

"I see. And you have other bids?"

"I do."

"May I see what you have and decide whether I can afford to raise them?"

"Nothing's written down; it's all verbal."

"Then will you tell me the amount of the highest offer?"

He named a figure more than three times what she had paid to UET; she was certain he lied.

"And does that include the freeze-chamber?"

Tregare scowled and moved a hand, negating. "No freeze on here; the damned things aren't working right. Unreliable."

"And how long—subjective time—is the trip?"

His grin tilted. "You think I give out that information? Figure about a year, and you won't be too disappointed either way."

She had almost decided to drop the matter and leave when Osallin spoke. "Did I forget to mention, Captain Tregare, that Ms. Obrigo is a Hulzein protégée? I believe you occasionally do business with Hulzein agents, other than myself?"

"Yeah." Tregare nodded. "Okay—half of what I just told you. But no less."

She could not resist asking, "What about the other bidders?"

Tregare scowled at her. "What you do on this ship is ride it. What you don't do is ask questions. You got it?"

Again she wavered; did she want to travel under this man's jurisdiction? Then adrenaline rose to his challenge and spoke for her. "I always ask questions. Everywhere. But I agree—you have the right not to answer. And so do I."

His smile surprised her. "We lift day after tomorrow, around sunset. Bring your gear aboard two hours early. No time for last-minute stuff; you see?"

"I understand." Tregare's hand waved dismissal; the two left his quarters and made their way off the ship.

In the ground car, moving toward Second Site, Osallin said, "Are you sure, Tari?"

"No. Of course not. But I am going."

YOUNG RISSA

● ● ●

THE morning of her departure date, Rissa coded a report for Erika—or Frieda—Hulzein. In particular, she directed that her UET holdings be increased. Shortly after noon, she checked out of the First Ever, finding more warmth in Charling's handshake and "Good luck, Ms. Obrigo" than she had expected.

Osallin accepted her report, promised to forward it "soonest" and drove her to the port. At the foot of *Inconnu*'s ramp they stood for a moment; he held out his hand. "I wish you well, Tari."

She took the hand in both of hers. "And I you, Osallin." Then she flung her arms around his neck and kissed him. Her tears overflowed. "Only now I realize—will I ever see you again? And you have been like—"

"An arm of Erika. She has a long reach."

"And a warm one, comforting. A person needs friends—I have had very few. Good-bye, Osallin. Whenever I send for anything for you to relay to the Hulzeins, there will be a personal message also."

"I'll do the same. Here—do that again—the kiss." She did, then turned and carried her belongings up into *Inconnu*.

ENTERING the ship she saw Tregare, several paces from where she stood, shaking his head at the group that surrounded him. She thought, *this is no time to bother him,* and walked slowly along the corridor she remembered. At the first cross-juncture she was accosted by a young woman wearing frayed UET uniform coveralls.

"You the new passenger?"

"Yes. Where should I put my luggage?" Rissa looked at the girl—about her own age and height but built more sturdily—a dark Caucasian type with strong cheekbones under close-cut curling hair, and a heavy jaw.

"I dunno. The galley for now, maybe—sit and have coffee.

Come on." Rissa followed, sat and accepted a cup of strong, rank coffee. The girl left.

Two sips was all the coffee Rissa wanted. She sat while it cooled and for a time after, while the bench she sat on lost what comfort it first had. When the girl returned, Rissa was both relieved and irritated.

"Come on. Captain says you come with me." The girl did not offer to help carry Rissa's belongings. She led her to Tregare's quarters.

Explosively, Rissa exhaled. "What *is* this? Why must I carry my gear from one place to another, where I will not be staying?"

Tregare's voice answered; Rissa had not heard him approach. "You're staying here, Ms. Obrigo. The rest of the ship is full."

Before Rissa could protest, the dark girl spoke. "So where do *I* go?"

Tregare laughed. "No place, Chira—you stay right here. We're going to have a lot of fun together."

Chira spat. "I don't do that stuff. You know that—I *don't*."

Rissa thought, *I need this girl on my side.* "Neither do I," she said. "Do not worry." *Sometimes one must lie.* She turned to Tregare. "I have bought passage—only that. Or else I leave this ship."

He reached out a long arm, clenched his fingers in her hair and slowly shook her head from side to side. She thought, *I would have to kill him. And I need this ride.* Breathing deeply, holding back from any action, she waited to hear what he would say.

"Nobody's getting off—and here's where you're staying, all right. Don't try to crap me up about how you don't do this or that, either; I know the Hulzein training program. You got it?"

"Let go of my hair." When he did, she both-hands brushed it back before saying, "Erika has more than one training program."

He laughed. "I know," he said, and left the quarters.

Chira spoke. "You try take that sonbitch away from me, I

break you some arms and legs. I—"

"Chira! *I* do not want him. I may have to accept him to some extent; I do not know. But I am not your rival or enemy."

"You better not! I break you."

Impatient, Rissa shook her head. "Forget that. I—I fight good, Chira."

"Maybe, maybe not. If you do, why be friends?"

"Why not? And why do you want to keep—that sonbitch, you said?"

"He gives me—a place, here. Not down below, one of the property."

Rissa shuddered. "Property? This ship is worse than I thought."

"Worse than I figured, too, when I got on. Hey—you mean it—friends?"

"I mean it, Chira."

"Me too, then. Look—we drink on it, with Tregare's best booze!" Chira rummaged in a drawer, brought out a key and unlocked a glass-fronted liquor cabinet. Glasses poured, the two toasted each other.

LIFTOFF caught Rissa unaware. She had expected a warning announcement and a period of heavy acceleration; instead the process was unheralded, noisy and relatively gentle. Around her the ship vibrated, then slowly quieted.

"Out of atmosphere now," said Chira. Rissa nodded. A silent pause lengthened. Then Tregare entered.

"Inspection time." He gestured toward Rissa's luggage. "Open 'em up." *Is this the time to defy him? No—not yet.* She complied. He searched skillfully, she thought—but did not discover any of the built-in hiding places. He held up the lock box Osallin had obtained for her. "Open it."

Now was the time; she shook her head. "That is private —Hulzein business."

"All the more reason. I'm in on a lot of Hulzein business, myself."

"Not on this; I have my instructions. Why, *I* cannot open the thing."

He looked at the box, then back to her. "You almost lie like a Hulzein—but not quite."

She shrugged. "Believe what you wish. I cannot oblige you."

He turned the box over in his hands. "Photolock, isn't it? An old trick." He put one hand to her nape, holding her, and brought the box to her eyes. "Keep 'em open!" She did; the scanner, seeing the plastic-aided patterns of Tari Obrigo, did not respond. Tregare released her. "Somebody else's pattern, then," he said. "Well, I've opened photolocks before."

"If you try to open this one, do it somewhere else. Or let me out of here—and Chira, also."

"Booby-trapped, is it? That's fine; you can tell me how."

Rissa evaded his reach. "You know Erika better than that. Would she allow me to be a possible weak link? I have no idea what the protection is. It could be any of fifty ways—you know that, if you stop to think."

"Yeah." He scratched his head. "All right—if it's set up that tricky, maybe it's out of my league anyway. And if you can't open it yourself, I don't have to worry you've got a weapon in there."

She laughed. "Is that what you were afraid of?"

His lips twitched; he raised a hand but lowered it without striking her. "Afraid? Don't use that word to me, you bitch!"

His reaction shocked her. *Has he so much fear that he cannot stand even to hear the word?* But she said, "Why not, you bastard?"

This time he did slap her. Trained, she moved enough to take the sting out. "I see," she said. "You can call names but I cannot? This is hardly a good beginning for a friendly relationship."

His face relaxed; then came his lopsided grin. "Friendly, eh? All right—let's see you be friendly."

Without answering, she stood and removed her clothing. "You see? No weapons on my person, either." She lay supine on the larger of the two beds and slowly, deliberately, flexed her knees to raise and spread her legs.

"Very well," she said, "let us get on with it. What are you waiting for?"

His mouth opened; he licked his lips. "You know something? You're not a very *feminine* woman, are you?"

"I did not have a very feminine upbringing. I am as I am."

"Yeah—well, we'll see." He stripped—the scars on limbs and body startled her—and was ready immediately. Without preliminary, so that briefly she felt pain, he plunged at her like a bull—no finesse or technique, only a rhythmic pounding. Angered, she had impulse to use words and motions she knew to deflate his potency. Then she thought better of it and began to move so as to slow him, to vary his movements and prolong the act. When he climaxed, bellowing like that same bull, he lay spent.

Eventually he pushed himself up and sat. "You didn't come?"

"I seldom do."

"You didn't even fake it—try to make me feel good."

"That, I *never* do." *I would not give you the satisfaction.*

"Chira does. She does it real good—don't you, Chira?"

The girl pouted. "I do better than her. Anytime, Tregare."

"Yeah? Well, not right now. Go get us all something to eat."

"*You*, sure, Tregare. She can get her own."

Even tired, he moved like a cat. His slap knocked Chira skidding. "You forgetting how to take orders?" He stalked toward her.

Rissa leaped and caught his arm. "No, Tregare! She is upset, that is all. Wait, Chira—I will clothe myself and come with you, to help. We must share these chores; I may as well start learning."

The man looked at her. "Ms. High-and-Mighty Paying Passenger wants to help with the scutwork?"

"If you call it scutwork to accommodate one another in these small matters—then yes."

"Oh, get the hell out of here. And hurry it up—I'm hungry."

She returned his gaze. "It would serve you right if we ate in the galley and *then* brought your food. Cold."

His mouth began a snarl—then he laughed. "Talk all you want, Obrigo. You know better than to do it."

DINNER relaxed them all. Afterward, over wine, Tregare became talkative. "What all did Osallin tell you about me?"

Rissa shrugged. "What is there to tell? So far as we know, you command the only armed ship ever to Escape. It is said that sometimes you use your armaments as threat to bilk your suppliers, groundside. And that your command came not as consequence of Escape, but afterward. And—"

He interrupted. "That old mutiny story, is it? Well, it wasn't how you think."

Her brows raised. "So? Then how was it, Tregare?"

He drained his glass, poured another and leaned forward. His face showed strain. "Obrigo? You know how ships Escape? You risk death, is how. People—officers, especially —who want out of UET—they talk, feel each other out. You think you have enough on the right side, you make your move. . . ."

His eyes narrowed; Rissa saw that they looked beyond her. Tregare said, "It's better if the captain's with you, but old Rigueres was UET all the way—not a chance. So Monteffial— he was First Hat, I was Third—he cut Rigueres' throat and we had the ship. But we'd made some bad guesses; there were more against us than we thought. And Farnsworth—Second Hat—he was playing double agent, pretending he was with us and planning to hang us with UET.

"He had Monteffial killed—didn't have the guts to do it himself—got most of our people locked up and set course for Earth. Where he missed—" Now Tregare laughed. "Where he missed, was with me. I'd gone outside in a power suit to fix a viewscreen input—communications was my specialty—and hadn't logged the jaunt.

"So Farnsworth didn't know I was out, didn't know Deverel was covering for me at the airlock, and told me the scoop when I came in. So I didn't take off the power suit, was all. I walked right through Farnsworth's goons with their knives and such, and caught him and broke his neck. And turned our people loose. The rest—the UET holdouts—went outside without suits. And that's your mutiny. Not against our Escape command—against a UET takeover. And I wrecked the suit doing it."

His face was flushed. He drained his glass and tapped it on the table. Chira refilled it.

"That is most interesting, Tregare. It explains a great deal."

"Like what?"

"Such as—well, an experience of that sort must not be easy to live with. I will remember and make allowances."

His laugh was half a snort. "Nobody has to make allowances for Tregare. On this ship *I* make the allowances. Don't forget that."

"Very well," said Rissa. She smiled.

She thought he would hit her, but after a moment he laughed, and this time freely. "You're a smart one, aren't you, Obrigo—I'll keep that in mind."

"And I will keep in mind, Tregare, that you are another."

SHIP'S time was measured by Earth days, but Rissa had no need to keep count. In her lock box an isotope-powered watch steadily noted, on its calendar dials, the subjective duration of her passage days. Those days were much alike—she ate, slept, visited various parts of the ship, and feigned lack of interest in the knowledge she eagerly accumulated.

She asked no questions; she waited until the answers came unasked, to fill gaps in her growing expertise. At turnover, in the control room, fidgeting and pretending boredom, she learned the location of Number One. Mentally she filed that answer with the rest.

• • •

F. M. Busby

SHE had little converse with Tregare's officers and less with the crew. She suspected that he had ordered it so, but did not accuse nor ask him.

In the case of First Officer Gonnelsen, no such stricture was needed. Except in line of duty, Rissa never heard him speak. Yet he seemed relaxed and calm; when he did talk, his voice was low and pleasant.

Third Officer Hain Deverel always greeted her with a smile. But the short, dark-haired man did not follow the greeting with talk, so neither did Rissa.

The one who did speak without constraint was Second Officer Zelde M'tana—a tall, very black woman, large-boned— but with her considerable height, slender in appearance. At first sight the woman startled Rissa—her strongly pronounced features, the tightly curling hair cut to a close-fitting cap, the deep voice when she spoke. From her left ear dangled a large heavy gold ring; on the right side, the lobe was missing.

Caught staring, Rissa felt herself flush. The other said, "The ear? Bandits—they used to be bad, in the back alleys of Parleyvoo. That's on Terranova."

"I—I am sorry—I did not intend rudeness. Even though you are very striking, still I—"

The woman laughed. "I've been catching double takes ever since I got my growth. You're Tari Obrigo, aren't you? I'm Zelde M'tana—Second Hat." Her hand engulfed Rissa's smaller one, but her grip was gentle.

"I am pleased to know you, Second Officer M'Tana."

"Make it Zelde, will you?" Rissa nodded. "Those bandits, though—out of the dark, two grabbed me and before I knew it a third one sliced my ear to get the gold. Lucky he didn't get the whole ear—I guess I jerked sideways enough so he missed."

"And then—how did you get away?"

"Me?" Zelde laughed. "I didn't get away—and only one of *them* did. Bad luck, the one with the gold and part of my ear. I killed the other two, right enough."

The woman was smiling; Rissa smiled also. "I am glad you did."

YOUNG RISSA

"Yeah? Most people don't care for that part of the story. Tari—I think I *like* you."

AT a later meeting—in the galley and by chance—Zelde asked, "You have any plans for yourself, on the ship here?"

"I—what do you mean?"

"Just what I said. I started as captain's doxy myself. Not much future in it, I figured, on the long haul—so I learned things, how to help run a ship and all, and now I'm somebody in my own right. You could be, too—so think on it."

"Yes. Thank you. But I will not be on *Inconnu* much longer. My passage is to Number One."

"Passage? You're a *paid* passenger?" Rissa nodded, and the other burst into laughter. "That Tregare! Who else could work it to collect passage money from his bedmate?" She shook her head, then sobered. "I shouldn't make fun, Tari. And from the look of you, you're not beaten down or anything. Maybe I ought to mind my own business."

"No, Zelde—I appreciate your concern. But truly, I am all right."

As time passed, she lay less often with Tregare. Once only, by apparent accident, she destroyed his desire moments short of climax. Thereafter, though obviously she was more skilled than Chira, he approached her seldom—and never without taking pains to soften her mood. She in turn was careful not to allow him to ingratiate himself too easily. Once he looked at her and said, "If I thought you were playing games with me . . ."

She laughed. "We all play games—it is our nature."

"I don't."

"Of course you do. You are playing one now. The name of it is 'I don't play games.'"

One side of his mouth smiled. "You should have been a

space captain. Or, no—a politician.''

"Perhaps I shall be—a politician, I mean. On Number One.''

"I ought to put you outside without a suit—and the Hulzeins be hanged.''

"Perhaps you should. *Before*, though?'' In bed she held him incompleted long enough to see worry in his face; then brought him to jubilating, draining conclusion. For the first time she thought, *I must keep in touch with this man—he is dangerous, but I can handle him. He could be useful. Later* . . .

THE three sat at their last dinner; morning would see *Inconnu* landed. "This wine is special,'' said Tregare. "I save it for arrivals, and I have only enough for three more.''

"It is delicious,'' said Rissa. "I hope you can replenish your supply.''

"Not hardly, he can't.'' Chira laughed. "Comes from—I forget the name—UET's main base, off Earth. Armed ships there all the time, he says.''

" 'Stronghold,' it's called,'' said Tregare. "I got in and out of there once with fake papers. For repairs. That trick won't work a second time. But you never know—someday I may try the place again, at that.''

Rissa nodded. "Yes, you might. With a few more armed ships . . .''

He stared at her. "What have you heard?''

"Nothing specific. But you have taken another Escaped Ship—perhaps more? Obviously you wish to build your own fleet. Does your plan involve taking more armed UET ships, or arming your own?''

His voice was low. "Nothing's safe from you, is it? All right—either, or both. I have—well, never mind *that*—I—''

"You have someone trying to duplicate this ship's weapons; I guessed that much. I will not ask where. But the missing projector unit—the place I saw, where it used to be—you did not remove it for repairs, I think, because the defective freeze-chambers are still in place. And *why*, may I ask? You should—"

"Hey! You trying to tell me how to run my ship?"

"Someone should!"

His face reddened; his palm struck the table hard enough to rock the wine in its glasses. "Damn it, Obrigo—you're right again! I'll get those useless chambers off here as soon as we land."

"But maintain ownership; it may be they can be restored."

"I know that! Why don't you tell me how to zip my own shoes?"

Chira giggled. "You sure let her get you mad a lot."

He turned on the girl, then looked to Rissa and shook his head. "You're giving her bad habits—you know that?"

Rissa shook her head. "I do not consider honesty a bad habit. Impractical sometimes, but not bad."

Not quietly, Tregare exhaled. "Funny thing, Tari Obrigo. Like she says, you do get me mad. But—you know? I'll miss you."

For over a month he had not touched her. Now was the last night. Making her decision, she reached for his hand. "Tregare?"

"Yes?"

"At the first of this trip, I hated your guts."

"Come to that, I wasn't too crazy about yours. So?"

"Now—Tregare, I am not sure if I *like* you or not—or whether anyone should—but you are important to me. I want you to survive and succeed."

"Same to you and many of 'em. Anything else, while you're at it?"

"Yes, Tregare. Will you sleep with me tonight?"

And with skills she had never before shown him, she made that night one he would remember. And then lay wondering why her own body would not respond. For this time she had truly wanted him.

• • •

WHEN Chira woke her, Tregare was gone. "We're landed."

"Oh." Rissa sat up. "I had better get my things together and leave." She dressed and packed; the tasks took little time. Chira left and returned with their breakfasts.

"Your last eats on *Inconnu*."

Rissa sat and began eating. "Thank you, Chira."

"Y'welcome, Tari." The girl frowned. "First I didn't like you—you scared me. But you treat me good. I dunno—if you stayed on, pretty soon Tregare don't need me—I'm down with the property. But still—I'm gonna miss you."

Rissa moved around the table and hugged the girl. "Just remember, Chira—he does *not* own you. Stand up for yourself."

"I think I see it—yeah. Like the way you do, with him. Not too much, but sometimes."

"Perhaps now, Chira, he will be easier with you."

"Maybe. Hey—siddown, eat, before it gets all cold." Rissa obeyed. Then she brushed her hair—on the ship she had not bothered to curl it—and tied it back with a clasp.

When she was ready to leave, she carried all her gear. Chira said, "Tregare wants to see you, say good-bye before you get off."

"All right, I will." Laden, no hands free, she smiled good-bye as she left Chira to whatever destiny the girl could manage.

She looked for Zelde M'tana, then remembered the watch schedule; the woman would be sleeping. Near the main airlock she found Tregare arguing loudly with persons she had never seen—groundsiders here, she thought.

She waited briefly, then spoke. "Tregare—before I leave, do you have a moment?" Against the others' words his arm swung like a scythe; he came to her.

"So you're getting off. All done with me." His arm went round her shoulders.

"Getting off—yes. Done with you, Tregare? Will that not depend on our travels, yours and mine? If I settle here, I might be old before you next return."

He looked away from her. "You know, I could like that. I'd take you to bed and *you'd* be the grateful one."

She laughed and nipped his earlobe. "Do not bet on it. But stay in communication when you can. I shall when *I* can. And good luck, Tregare."

She left the ship and walked out into Number One's hot morning sunlight.

AT ground level an armed woman, an albino, met her. Rissa judged her insignia at officer grade. The woman said, "Identity check—get it all out, and tell me your reasons for coming here."

Rissa produced Tari Obrigo's papers. "Here are my bona fides." She paused and decided to chance it. *At the least, I may gain information.* "My presence on Number One concerns the Hulzein Establishment."

The pink eyes looked at her. "You're a Hulzein employee?"

"A . . . representative, you might say. I bring word from Earth and from the Far Corner connection."

The woman nodded; her white hair swung. "At this point, that's good enough. Come with me. I'll advise the Provost that you're coming."

A LARGE radius and low density gave Number One a gravity pull slightly less than Earth's. From the clumsy, jerky goundcar, Rissa watched scudding masses of purple cloud cover and uncover the sun. The ride was short. The driver—a burly man who had not spoken—led her into a windowless gray building, past a bank of elevators and up one flight of stairs, to a door labeled "Provost."

"In there," he said, and turned to leave.

She said, "Thank you." He did not answer. She took one deep breath, opened the door, entered, and closed the door behind her.

The walls simulated a jungle scene; play of shadows on

moving foliage had a hypnotic quality. Three persons were in the room but her attention went to the big dark-bearded man behind the largest desk—with the marker "Stagon dal Nardo: Provost." Even sitting, he loomed.

He cleared his throat and said, "Anyone can push the Hulzein name this far. Now let's see you back it up." He looked through the papers she handed him. "Tari Obrigo, eh?" He pronounced it AHB-riggo.

"Oh-BREEgo."

"Whatever . . ." He frowned. "Are you Hulzein-connected by blood? By marriage?"

"Neither."

"Then which Hulzein do you represent?"

She said, "None directly, Provost dal Nardo. I—"

"None directly, you say?" He tugged at his short, full beard. "That poses problems."

"I know Erika and Frieda. You have heard of them?"

"They're on Earth; you're here." He placed his hands flat on his desk, fingers spread. "Obrigo, so far you haven't convinced me you're more valuable alive than as fertilizer. Your status puts you under my jurisdiction—and we're very short of fertilizer."

She nodded; push had come to shove. "You are long on bullshit, if that helps. I pose problems? Then refer me to someone who understands them. You waste your time as well as mine—and I would like to get on with my business here."

He sneered. "Yours? I thought it was the Hulzeins'. The more you talk, the more I smell fertilizer."

She hadn't wanted this conflict—*damn the man!*—but now there was no evading it. Thinking quickly, she said, "It annoys me, having to deal in threats—but you leave no choice. Dal Nardo—are you immunized against zombie gas?"

His eyes widened. "I never heard of it. What—?"

She nodded. "I am not surprised. But in that case, I suggest you do not threaten me again." He said nothing. "Now, may we stop niggling and get on with it?"

"A moment." He glared at a subordinate. "I'll have to call and ask."

"Yes," she said. "That is the difference between us."

YOUNG RISSA

He spoke into a hushphone. *Zombie gas,* she thought—*I will have to remember that one!* But the fear she saw, plain on the faces of dal Nardo's aides, disturbed her.

DAL NARDO escorted her downstairs; outside, an aircar waited. Her previous escorts had helped with her luggage; he did not. He pointed to the car and walked away. Then he turned back briefly, to say, "You won't be around long, Hulzeins or no Hulzeins. That mouth of yours will have you dead on the dueling grounds. Perhaps by me." He entered the building, and Rissa moved to the aircar.

The pilot was a tall girl, Rissa's age or perhaps younger. Short, tousled hair showed fair around the edges of her jaunty cap. She smiled and said, "What's snicking the Provost? Wouldn't you spread for him?"

Despite her mood, Rissa smiled back. "He did not ask me—and just as well, too. No—do not get out—I can hoist these things in well enough." She did, and climbed in also—standing for a moment, wondering which seat to take.

"Here—come sit alongside me. You'll have a better view." Rissa joined her and fastened the safety harness, puzzled briefly by its unfamiliar design. The aircar took off and gained altitude rapidly. Its propulsion system made only a heavy soft hissing sound.

Rissa said, "You know dal Nardo, I take it."

The girl shook her head. "Only by reputation—and that's snooky with me."

Snooky also? Local slang, of course. "I would prefer that for myself also, I think—uh . . ."

The girl looked at her sidelong. "Oh—my name? Felcie—Felcie Parager. Dumb name, huh? What got the Provost knucking at you, anyway? Or can you say? And what's *your* name? Where are you from?"

In her mind Rissa ordered the stream of questions. "I am Tari Obrigo. From Far Corner, most recently. Any name is fine unless you yourself dislike it—if you do, then change it.

Yes, I can say how I offended dal Nardo. He began our interview by threatening my life, and I topped his threat; that is all."

Felcie laughed without restraint, then sobered. "I hope nobody else was there!"

"There were. Two of his aides."

"Then I'm afraid you've made a dangerous enemy. What did you snick him with, anyway?"

"Now, that I *cannot* tell you—sorry, Felcie."

The girl nodded. "Nothing shaken—we all have our secrets, don't we?" She pointed ahead. "Hill country coming up. We go alongside the first ridge maybe half an hour, then cross it at the Gap."

Rissa looked. At first the rolling, wooded hills seemed familiar, Earthlike—then she saw their gigantic scale. "On Earth, these would be called mountains."

"I know—I've heard. The Big Hills are oversize, like Number One itself."

"Were you born here, Felcie?"

"If you call it that. I'm one of the zoom-womb babies, hatched out of sperm and ova from a hijacked UET ship."

"I have heard of that episode—but I thought it was longer ago."

The girl laughed again. "Well, they couldn't hatch us all at once, you know. I'm from the last batch." Her face and voice turned serious. "Tari—what's it like to have parents—your own, I mean, instead of maybe one grownup to fifty or sixty kids?" After a silence she turned to look at Rissa.

"Did I say something?"

Rissa shook her head. "No, Felcie—it is merely that I do not know. It has been so long—I cannot really remember."

THE lodge clung to the edge of a high valley, overlooking a wooded downward sweep. Felcie landed in a clearing alongside the building. "I'll help you to the door with your things, but I'm not supposed to go inside. Comes to that—officially I don't even know who lives here.''

"Then I will not ask. So I cannot give you away by error."

"But *you* know, don't you? I mean—" Suddenly Felcie grinned and snapped her fingers; then her expression was solemn. "*Now* I know why the Provost . . ."

"Yes? Tell me."

"I should've stitched it together sooner." Her head gestured toward the lodge. "These people here—they don't win popularity contests among their rivals, but generally they're respected. Dal Nardo, though—it's common knowledge—he's a hating man, and anyone connected here is what he hates most."

"I . . . see. I wish I had known." Rissa shuddered briefly. "Well, perhaps I should go inside."

They disembarked. At the lodge's door the girl said, "I hope I see you again, Tari."

"So do I. And thank you." Rissa saw her walk away, and turned to the door and knocked.

THE young man who answered wore a hood and dark goggles. From his pale skin Rissa suspected he was another albino, and wondered if the condition were common on Number One. He said, "I'm Castel. And you're who?"

"Tari Obrigo."

His smile showed smallish teeth. "The one who angered Provost dal Nardo."

"I am afraid so. I would have preferred not to, but—"

"Dal Nardo's a frunk. But it's dangerous to provoke him— especially for a Hulzein connection lacking immune status. He hates this clan."

"So I have been told. But unfortunately, after the fact. And the way he talked, it seems dangerous even to meet him."

Castel shrugged. "I'm not standing in line for the privilege." He took one of her suitcases, turned and motioned for her to follow.

They walked down a wide hall paneled in dark wood. Castel

opened a carved door and gestured her inside. "Wait here. Sit facing the big chair." She nodded; he set the suitcase beside her and closed the door.

Before sitting she looked around the room—spacious but low-ceilinged, with heavy beams that matched the massive effect of its furnishings. Outside, climbing vines obscured the single large window and dimmed incoming sunlight. On the walls hung trophy heads of unfamiliar animals. The great chair, heavy and ornately carved, sat with its back near the window.

She heard a sound behind her and turned; a tall woman entered. Rissa gasped. "*Erika!*" But no—it could not be—the face was uncannily the same, but *younger* than Erika had been. And the thick braids, coiled crowning the head, were iron-gray, not white. "Frieda?" Yet she recalled Frieda's features as coarser, not so cleanly cut.

"Weren't you told to sit, Tari Obrigo? Please do so." The woman waited while Rissa seated herself facing the commanding position of the big chair, then walked to it and sat. Against the light Rissa could not see the face clearly, nor its expression. The woman chuckled. "You've pretty well established your bona fides. You knew Erika? And Frieda? What word do you bring me?"

"I knew them, yes. And their man on Far Corner."

"His name?"

"Osallin." The woman nodded, and Rissa said, "But who are *you?*"

"Erika didn't tell you? Then why are you here? Maybe our interview won't be as routine as I thought."

"Erika told me nothing of this planet. All that she—or I—knew of my plans was that I would go to Far Corner and then to whatever Hidden World I could reach. Osallin mentioned a Hulzein connection here on Number One. But you—you *are* a Hulzein, are you not?"

"What year did you leave Earth? How old was Erika?"

Rissa named the year. "She was seventy, and Frieda thirty."

"It matches." The nod took the crown of braids into and then out of a shaft of sunlight. "And what's your own age?"

"Biological? About eighteen, I think. I can say more closely from the day-count of my timepiece which is . . . packed away. And—what Earth year is it *now?*" Seeing the woman's smile, Rissa flushed and rephrased her question. "Yes—I know that simultaneity cannot apply over the distances we travel. But how old would I be, had I remained on Earth?"

"That's still not entirely accurate, but better. Let's see— about forty-four, I'd guess. Me, now—I'm a biological sixty, and twenty-nine years ahead of the game." She sighed. "If Erika's still alive, which I doubt, she'd be ninety-eight. And apparently she hadn't heard from me when you left—or didn't see fit to tell you, if she had."

After a moment Rissa said, "I do not know which." She shook her head. "You look so much like Erika. Younger, of course . . ."

"How long did you know her?"

"Something over a year. She . . . taught me."

For a moment, silence. Then; "You sound right; I'll take the chance. Not much of one—you don't leave the Lodge until I say so, and my jurisdiction's as absolute as Erika's. You understand?"

"Of course. But still I do not know—"

"Who I am? I'm Liesel Hulzein, Erika's sister."

"She said nothing—"

"She wouldn't. Well, then—tell me what you know of the Hulzeins."

"I know of Heidele, Renalle, Erika, and Frieda." She decided not to mention Osallin's forebodings. "But I did not know of you."

Liesel Hulzein rubbed a palm across her eyes. "No? Well, it's simple enough. Erika was a sickly child, so our mother had me—for insurance, continuity of the line. Erika and I got along all right until our mother died—the same year you were born, in fact. Then—it seems Hulzeins can't share power."

"And—what happened?"

"There was a showdown, and Erika won. She could have had me killed, but it turned out that Hulzeins don't kill each other, either. So she did what I'd have done in her place—let me get off Earth with fifty million Weltmarks as my share of the Establishment, and kept the rest. She said maybe we could trade together, or our children could, when I found a good base of operations. I doubt she realized—I didn't—it'd take thirty objective years to find one—*this* one. Frozen like a shrimp, I was, twenty-nine of those years."

The concept awed Rissa. Perhaps sixty years for round-trip communication? Only the long Hulzein view could work on such terms. She said, "From Earth to Far Corner I had a freeze-chamber. Then, coming here, the ship's chambers were inoperative, unsafe. But it was only a few months, biological."

Abruptly she decided to trust this woman. "Just a moment; I can tell you the exact time lapse." From a hidden recess in one suitcase she took a small device, used it at each eye, and unveiled her own gray irises. Then she held the lock box to her face; she blinked twice, and it opened. The calendar of her isotope-powered watch gave its answer. "Biologically," she said, "I have lived two hundred seventy-five days since boarding *Inconnu* at Far Corner."

"Inconnu?" The word came as a gasp.

"Yes. You know that ship?"

"I've heard of it. Go on."

"Oh. And—umm—of the time since I left Earth—and with the slowing of body-time by freezing—today I am biologically as near eighteen years old as makes no difference."

The older woman cleared her throat. "Fine. But something interests me more. Those little things you lifted off your corneas—far as I know, they don't work in more than one layer, so I'm seeing your real eye color. And it doesn't match with your identification. You call yourself Tari Obrigo—who are you, really?"

"The name should not matter, here—Rissa Kerguelen—you would not have heard it."

After a moment, Liesel pointed a finger. "Oh, but I have! —and not too long ago, from a fast ship Escaped direct from Earth. You're the child who won the Committee's lottery and skipped out, leaving UET grinding its teeth. So you went to ground at Erika's, did you? Now how did you manage that, fresh out of Welfare?"

"I had help—a friend of my parents."

"I see. And you were with Erika a year or so . . ." She paused. "Turn the lights on, will you? The switch is by the door." Rissa did so. Now, as she sat again, she could see the other's expression.

Smiling, Liesel Hulzein said, "I read what you said to the press the day you got out of Welfare. They asked what you planned to do, and you said—get off Earth, grow your hair down to your butt, and the rest was none of their business!" She laughed, coughed, then laughed again. "Well, you're off Earth, all right—the hair still has some way to go."

Self-consciously, Rissa reached to touch the ends of hair that lay against her back. "I have had less than three years, biological, and slowed for part of that time by the freeze-chamber. And I must trim the skimpy ends at the back to let the front catch up, or it does not look well."

Liesel's laugh was a whoop. "Oh, I wasn't trying to embarrass you. Just a factual comment because your remarks stuck in my mind. And I admired you for speaking up that way, under the circumstances." She gripped the arms of the big chair and came up standing.

"I'll have Castel show you to your room. Unpack, rest, have a bath—a snack, if you like; he'll bring you something. And be dressed to have dinner with us shortly after sundown."

"Us? And how shall I dress?"

"Us is whoever I have to table. Dress as you like."

HER room was on the third floor, at the front. Its window looked out over a vast sweep of woodland to the range of hills she had crossed. Here too, the walls were wood-paneled, but in a lighter color. The bath dwarfed Rissa; one faucet brought warm water that bubbled gently and smelled of forest. She lay a long time, head propped on a cushion so that face and ears were above water. Then almost in one motion she gripped the sides of the bath, drew her feet under her, and sprang erect. She felt refreshed, euphoric; without volition her laugh came.

She toweled herself. Then off came Tari Obrigo—the nose mole, the protruding teeth-cap, the fingerprints—all of it. She brushed back her wet hair, gripped the mass to bring the ends around to vision, and trimmed off a wispy half-inch. Then she dried it and held one mirror to see herself reflected in another. It was getting there, she thought—the front *was* catching up to the back. Still far short of her impromptu boast, but—oh, well . . .

ANOTHER young man—Ernol, taller than Castel and of African ancestry—summoned her for dinner and showed her the way. The dining room reminded her of the room in which she had met Liesel—the same effect of massiveness. Wall lights and a central chandelier were jets of burning gas.

Against a wall stood a huge table; under the central lights was placed a smaller one. It would have seated six, but only four chairs surrounded it.

Liesel sat in one. To her right was a younger woman—perhaps, by Earth years, nearing thirty—tall, slim, with dark hair coiled atop her head and a lean, tanned face. All her features were emphatic—heavy arched brows over green eyes, the cheekbones and chin, blade-straight nose over a wide mouth—it was, thought Rissa, as though her face competed with its own parts. And yet the whole had a precarious harmony.

The man at Liesel's left Rissa guessed to be nearly seven feet tall. A curly black beard largely hid his swarthy face. His eyes were deep-set; she could not determine their color.

Liesel glanced up and said, "Do sit down. Rissa Kerguelen, be acquainted with Hawkman and Sparline Moray." The two nodded but said nothing; Rissa did the same, and sat.

Young persons brought food and wine; the wall lights dimmed and went dark. "There is a business matter," said Hawkman Moray in a soft, deep voice. "Fennerabilis over-reaches himself."

"When he loses his balance," said Liesel, "we push. Sparline—could you distract his attention for a time at the next ten-day gathering?"

"So long as I need not give him mine, *after* the gathering."

As the discussion began, excluding Rissa, so it continued. Trying to follow it, she ate without noting flavors. Time passed slowly; she was filled, but continued eating for want of anything else to do. Her one attempt at conversation, a comment on her impressions of the planet, was not only ignored but interrupted.

All right, she thought; she could sulk with the best of them. She kept silence and soon was engrossed in her own thoughts, unheeding of the talk that so pointedly ignored her. *I do not have to stay here*, she thought. *I can play docile for a time, and then* . . . After all, she still had Cele Metrokin as a hole card—and Laura Konig. At the time for drugsticks, she smoked automatically and lightly.

Liesel's voice cut through her preoccupation. "I *said*, 'Rissa—we're not boring you, are we?' "

She shook her head, not in negation but to clear her mind. She said, "It is futile to lie to a Hulzein, and I prefer the truth anyway. You are boring the hell out of me, and you all very well know it."

Hawkman Moray grunted, touched a napkin to his lips, and rose. "In that case we will desist. Come, Sparline."

The woman stood also. "Good night, Liesel." Arm in arm, the two left the room.

Alarmed, Rissa looked at her hostess. "Should I follow and apologize?"

"No, they found out what they wanted to know. So did I."

"Have I made myself unwelcome here?"

Liesel shook her head. "You've missed the point. Rissa, did you understand anything of what was said here?"

Rissa started to say no, then realized that the gist had stuck in her mind. "It is a power play. Fenner—whatever his name is—is trying to undermine your influence in the Windy Lakes area. So you will use—oh, I forget the names—to give him trouble elsewhere, to occupy him while you sew the Lakes up solidly. And—"

"That's close enough. You see, you *did* understand. Then why were you bored?"

"Because no one ever *spoke* to me, or explained who anybody is. I—"

"In some ways, you're a spoiled child. Capable, yes—but untrained."

"*Erika* trained me!"

"In some skills. Not, apparently, in patience or subtlety." She waved a hand. "No, no—don't confuse individual guile with the ability to work subtly in group actions. However, I have hope for you—if you're willing to learn. And if you survive, once you're ready for work outside this place."

"Survive? Why should I not?"

"Dal Nardo. I called him—he wants your life, all right. He hates anything to do with the Hulzeins, and you humiliated him. He as much as told me I can't hide you forever—and when you come out, you'll be challenged by hired duelists."

Rissa's eyes narrowed. "Yes—at the last, he mentioned dueling." She smiled. "But why should I wait for him to try to hire me dead? Do you think—is he person enough to face me himself, or would he apologize to satisfy the customs and skulk behind paid killers?"

Liesel shook her head. "Dal Nardo never apologizes."

"Then would it disturb you if he dies?"

"You're crazy, girl! He's expert with blade and gun—and without them he'd break your neck between two fingers."

"Perhaps, perhaps not. I think not. Why not give me the chance?"

"Because—all right, Erika taught you and she's one of the best—*I* wouldn't want to fight you and believe me, I'm very good, for my age. But—you're so goddamned *young*. Why not wait—and hope to avoid trouble?"

"Liesel—*you* have no real faith in that possibility?"

For a moment the woman put her hands to her face. "No. No, I haven't." She reached for the wine bottle and poured them each a glass. "All right. When you—when *we're* ready, I'll arrange, if you still wish it, for you to challenge Stagon dal Nardo."

"Good." Rissa lifted her glass. "Let us toast that meeting."

Each drank. A silent pause lengthened; then Liesel said, "You have to know how things work here. We can't start to teach you any sooner."

"You mean, like your government? How *does* it work?"

If Liesel intended a smile, she failed. "In a word, badly. Not for most of the people; it treats them well enough. But it —I suppose you'd call it a benevolent oligarchy—is hamstrung by power struggles. We waste more time fighting each other than working for the benefit of the planet—let alone the other Hidden Worlds or the Escaped Ships."

One word stuck in Rissa's mind. "*We*, you said?"

"Certainly; I'm one of them. Thirty-seven families own everything of importance on Number One—land, maritime rights, business interests, what-have-you. There were nearly twice as many to start with, but the infighting got rid of the rest—as competitors, and sometimes literally. The dal Nardos, for instance, got their start in the assassination business."

Rissa thought. "No different from Earth, then—not really."

"I'm afraid you're right—we talk freedom and fight for power. I come by it honestly, by genetics and indoctrination both—I don't know what excuses the others make to themselves."

"About the same, I would expect," said Rissa. "But is there no cooperation among you?"

"Surely—when interests coincide. I try to work that way, when I can. But then along comes—well, Fennerabilis, say, and—"

"Yes. I remember the name now."

"I'm not having the man killed, mind you—he's doing a good job in his own sector, under tough circumstances. That's the tricky part, actually—stopping his power grab *and* keeping him alive."

"It's true," said Rissa, "that some are more worthy than others, to be kept living."

The older woman laughed, a harsh sound. "I like the way

you put that." Then her expression sobered. "One thing I haven't asked yet. Number One's like a chessboard and most people are pawns, if that. I need to know your rank on the board."

Rissa nodded. "By wealth, you mean?"

"Of course. While you can hold it."

Rissa told her—how much on Earth and how invested, how much with Osallin on Far Corner, and the sums she had brought with her. The other's lips moved silently.

Then Liesel said, "Twenty-seven years' appreciation of Earth assets, fifteen at Far Corner. With what you brought—well, if you live, Rissa Kerguelen, Number One has another oligarch."

THEY finished the wine; Rissa declined another round of drugsticks. Despite her training, her feet were less than steady as they left the dining room.

"I'll show you upstairs," Liesel said. "No point in rousing one of the help so late." Companionably they walked up to Rissa's room.

At the door, Rissa turned and said, "They make a handsome couple, the Morays."

Liesel Hulzein stared at her, then laughed. "*Couple?* Sparline's my daughter. And having seen Erika's Frieda and the failures before her, I didn't follow her example of letting the unassisted Hulzein genes go fuzzy around the edges. Hawkman Moray is Sparline's father."

Before Rissa could find answer, Liesel closed the door.

A YOUNGISH girl, perhaps fourteen, came to wake Rissa next morning. But daylight had roused her earlier—she lay, eyes open, thinking less of what she had learned than of what she had yet to learn. The girl said, "Pardon. Ms. Moray asks you to join her at breakfast."

"Thank you. Tell her I will be down shortly." Throwing

back the covers she swung her legs over, to stand in one fluid motion. The girl stared at her nudity, then turned and quickly left the room.

Rissa washed, brushed her hair and dressed. A few minutes later she found the same girl outside her door, waiting to lead her downstairs. Rissa followed, to a cheerful room that faced morning sun. At a small table Sparline Moray sat alone; before her were a glass of pale liquid and a steaming cup. Her hair was down, lying in loose waves against her vermilion robe.

She looked up. "I'm having some of our local fruit juice and Number One's version of coffee. Would you like some, before food's served?" She gestured toward two pitchers.

"Yes, please." She sat facing the other woman and filled the glass and cup at her place. "It is kind of you to invite me to join you."

"I wanted to talk to you." Sparline smiled. "More precisely, I still do."

"If it concerns last night," Rissa said, "—my rudeness—"

"Provoked by our own—to see how much string we could let out before you pulled it tight. No, no—nothing shaken."

"I am glad. Then what do you wish to talk about?"

"Tell me of yourself."

As she thought, Rissa sipped—the pale juice was both sweet and tart, the coffee much like Earth's. "What is it you would like to know?"

"Whatever you choose to tell. Your choices will tell me a lot, also."

"Very well—from the beginning. If I bore you, say so—and I will shorten the story." So—briefly, her birthplace, her parents and their deaths. A quick sketch—impersonal, as though she had been an observer—of life in Total Welfare. The lottery prize—Camilla Altworth, the year at Erika's—Far Corner and Osallin. ". . . then he found me passage here, to Number One. The first thing I did here was to find trouble with an egomaniac named dal Nardo. The second was to come to this place." Brows lifted, she waited.

Sparline nodded. "A little skimpy in spots, but quick and to the point. Well, enough for now—our meal's arriving."

Rissa sampled eggs, smaller than those she knew, a toasted bun and then another, and slices of grilled meats. She found she had good appetite. Neither spoke during the meal; then Sparline said, "More coffee?" Rissa nodded. "And I imagine you have some questions yourself. Ask away; if I'm not free to answer, I'll say so."

"That is fair. Well—this is only personal curiosity, Ms. Moray, but—you were born on Earth?"

"First names are correct between us, Rissa. To one of your status, I'm Sparline and my mother is Liesel."

Rissa laughted, not long. "I am not sure what my status is."

"Probational, of course, but tentatively one of *us*. If you don't prove out, you're free to make your own way—on Number One or elsewhere. In that case, I'd be Ms. Moray."

Rissa had no comment. Sparline said, "Now, your question—yes, I was born on Earth. Don't imagine that Erika approved—or my grandmother Renalle—when Liesel departed from Hulzein doctrine. But after two bad tries at parthenogenesis, she consulted a geneticist. Erika and Renalle both rejected his findings, so my mother went to manage family holdings on another continent—and there she chose Hawkman Moray, my father."

"She fell in love with him?"

"I don't think so—not then. But he stood with her against Erika's forces and helped bring her here—and now she values him above all other men."

Rissa thought. "And they had you. Why no others?"

"Have some more coffee." Sparline stared down at her cup, then said, "After me it wasn't possible—complications. But a year before me they also had a son."

"And is he here also?"

Sparline's tone was bitter. "Do you think the Hulzeins —Renalle and Erika—would accept male inheritance even partially? Liesel and Hawkman had to hide him—hide his very existence—or he'd have been killed. But I knew him until he was thirteen. He was good to me—I wouldn't begrudge him his half of what I have—or will have."

"But what happened? Do you know where he is?"

"Sometimes—but he won't have anything to do with us, in

person. Just business sometimes, through others.''

"I do not understand."

"It was a bad thing. To protect him, Liesel faked all his records; he was registered under his middle name, with fic-·titious parentage. Then when the showdown came with Erika, my parents had to move fast—they bought his way into UET's space academy. It's a nightmare, that place, but it was safe from Erika. Then we had to leave Earth—and there was no time or way to rescue him!"

Rissa saw Sparline shudder. "Horrible life, that—for a young boy with no protective influence backing him. We didn't know how bad by half until it was too late. It made him hard. His ship Escaped not long after he joined it—thank peace for that! But now he's called pirate and outlaw and mutineer by people who don't even know him!

"Poor Tregare!"

RISSA'S mind began and rejected one sentence after another. Finally; "He—he did not mutiny against his own people. UET had retaken the ship. He told me."

Sparline's mouth went slack, her face pale. For a moment her lips moved without sound. Then; "You were on *Inconnu*? It's here? Liesel didn't—" Her cup struck the table; coffee slopped over. She rose, took two fast strides, then returned and sat again. "No. He'll be here a week at least. It's more important now—what you can tell me of him." Her color returned. "*Tell* me, Rissa!"

"I rode *Inconnu* here from Far Corner—I thought you knew."

"Did you see much of Tregare? Did you come to know him well?"

Rissa did not allow the potential smile to move her mouth. "Over a journey of nine months, a little more? In some ways, quite well."

Sparline leaned forward. "What kind of man is he . . . now? Did you like him?"

Rissa sipped coffee. "He is—hard, as you said—on the surface, at least. He is sometimes violent and ruthless—but not so much as he likes to think he is. He has little regard for the rights or feelings of anyone he does not value personally. He is very able—but capable of overlooking important factors if his attention is caught elsewhere.

"Did I like him?" She shrugged. "At first I distrusted and almost feared him. Now I respect parts of his nature, and certainly his achievements. Between us there is both antagonism and a certain affection. Perhaps—" She sighed. "Let us say that I will be disappointed if I do not see him ever again."

Sparline shook her head slowly. "You know more of him than I do—and in less than a year. I envy you."

"You need not. I shared his quarters, not by my own choice."

Now the other's cheeks flushed; she gripped Rissa's arm. "You say my brother raped or enslaved you?"

Rissa spoke carefully. "No. He could not have done so—I was trained, remember, by Erika. To some extent he did coerce me. I accepted that coercion because the alternative was to kill him and fight my way off the ship. And I needed the ride."

"You? *You* couldn't kill Tregare!"

"I think I could have. No matter—I did not, and am glad of it."

Sparline scowled at her, then the scowl relaxed. "Yes—you said—a certain affection. You came to love him, didn't you?"

Rissa shrugged. "Not by my definition, but call it what you like. It is true that the last time we bedded, I invited him. Because it may have been our final night together, I let myself be sentimental."

Finally Sparline released her numbing grasp; Rissa flexed the arm. "All right—so my brother isn't the paragon I'd like to think him. But even though he first took you against your will—"

"Not against my will—against my inclination. There is a difference."

"Don't pick nits. With all that, I say—still you came to like him, admire him. Didn't you?"

Rissa nodded. "In our personal dealings, yes—as I have said. But in some other matters, no."

"What matters?"

"On *Inconnu*, I was told by one who should know, are women who are called 'property.' Can you like or admire the thought of human property?"

Sparline waved a hand. "A joke—it has to be. My brother wouldn't—"

Rissa stood. "Believe what you like. I was there; you were not. And I think it time I thanked you for your hospitality and excused myself."

Sparline stood also. "You're right." Her smile showed effort. "Rissa—I'm not angry. I'm sure you're telling the truth as you know it. But now I'm going to the port to try to see my brother for the first time in—it must be fifteen years, biological time. Later we can talk more."

"Will you give Tregare a message for me?"

"Sure, if I reach him. What is it?"

"That Tari Obrigo—he knows me only by that name—sends her regards. And—and holds no grudges."

"I'll be happy to tell him that—if you mean it."

"If I did not, I would not say so. Tregare and I—I feel—are even with each other. And both gained, perhaps."

"All right. If I can't see him, I'll try to leave word." Sparline left the room, and Rissa thought, *I wonder if he will bother to send answer.*

SHE found the way to her room, performed necessary functions, and lay on the bed for a time, considering what she and Sparline had said, and what might come of it. Her thoughts meandered into half-formed dreams, with little content except vague emotion. She dozed; a knock awakened her. "Come in!"

Liesel entered. "Did I wake you? Well, so be it—the sun's high, or was, until the clouds got here." She pulled a chair alongside the bed and sat. "Sparline seldom shouts at me. She did, though, before she made off with the only aircar that wasn't already in use. Do you know why?"

Rissa pushed her hair back and moved to sit on the edge of the bed. "I thought she knew *Inconnu* was here, that I had come on it. She was disturbed that you had not told her her brother is aground."

Liesel shook her head slowly. "You know a lot very quickly, don't you? That could be dangerous, and not only to yourself. What else do you know that I don't?"

"How should—I mean, how can I know?" Rissa stood; after a moment she put a hand, gently, to the older woman's shoulder. "I am new here—inexperienced in your ways—I have no way of knowing what secrets one Hulzein keeps from another. Nothing I said to Sparline was from malice or self-seeking."

Liesel covered Rissa's hand with her own. "Yes, child—I'm sure of that. But to the point—what did you tell her of Tregare? And she to you?"

Rissa bowed her head and raised it again. "Our exact words escape me. I will tell you what I remember, and of my association with Tregare, when I did not know he was one of you." The telling was not long; at the end, Liesel squeezed Rissa's hand, then released it. She stood.

"One thing I need to know. Could you be pregnant by my son?"

Rissa thought, *one secret I keep for a time yet. And I am not lying.* She laughed. "A Welfare child? You must know better."

"In a way I regret that; otherwise you reassure me. No damage is done if Sparline keeps her head, and she will. I appreciate your story of the mutiny; Tregare was always too proud to excuse his actions. How did *you* get it out of him?"

After thought, Rissa said, "He may have felt he owed me something."

"Maybe." Liesel had slouched; now she stood erect. "Well—I thank you for telling me. Now I've work to do. Would you like to walk outdoors, explore our grounds?" Rissa nodded assent. "Fine; I'll send someone to escort you. You'd better dress a little more warmly."

YOUNG RISSA

• • •

THE next knock was Hawkman Moray's. He smiled and held up a basket. "Peace offering. Would you like luncheon with me—up our valley an hour's walk?"

"Yes, of course. I will fetch my outergarb."

They left by a back door and walked up a winding path, through fragrant underbrush. Clouds purpled the sky, but the gentle climb warmed Rissa.

He was not really seven feet tall—but nearer seven than six. How old was he biologically? She would have taken him for Sparline's brother rather than father. She did not ask.

The climb grew steeper, wound between heavy thickets, then leveled abruptly; they entered a flowered clearing.

"This is the place." He moved to one side. "The view is best here," and he unfolded a covering to spread on the ground. In the middle he placed the basket, and sat beside it. "Are you hungry, Rissa? I am."

"Yes. The walk gave me appetite." She sat also, looking past him down the valley. Against the distant hills the great Lodge was a toy.

"Some wine first," he said, as he unpacked the basket. "And perhaps some talk?"

She stiffened. "Questions; right? Ask away—you can all compare notes later."

Hawkman Moray laughed; in the clearing the sound rang. "I'd thought to let you ask most of the questions."

She looked at him, at his broad smile. "I do not understand."

He poured red wine and handed her a glass. "There are several of us and only one of you. You have more to learn than we have."

He touched his glass to hers; they both sipped. "What does that mean?"

"Without asking you won't find out, will you?" His mouth twitched upward; she could not withhold an answering grin.

"Very well, Hawkman—Sparline tells me first names are in

order between us—I will ask. First, why does Sparline bear your name and not Liesel's? And did Tregare?''

Sitting tall before her, he shrugged. "These customs vary. You carry your mother's name, do you?"

"And my brother, my father's. Your customs were different?"

"A moment." From the basket he was filling two plates; he set one before her. "Let's eat while we talk. More wine?" He poured it. "In the ordinary case, our daughter would be a Hulzein."

"And your son?"

"Liesel told me of you and Tregare. He inherits my own early lack of self-discipline—perhaps I owe you an apology on his behalf."

She laughed. "Apologies are useless waste; the thing is over. But tell me of his naming."

"Our family also names sons for their fathers. He was Bran Tregare Moray until we had to hide him—then merely Bran Tregare."

"I knew him as Tregare, only. How—how old is he?"

"Biologically? I can't know—I don't know how much he's traveled. Chronologically, perhaps fifty-seven."

"Then he has traveled greatly. But what of Sparline's name?"

He was chewing; after he swallowed he said, "Hulzein heirs outside the main Establishment were prime targets. We felt she was safer under the inconspicuous name of Moray. We never changed it."

"I see. Hawkman—I do not know what this green paste is but I want more of it, if any is left, to put on my bread."

"Of course. A moment—I'll spread some for you."

"Thank you. Hawkman, how old are you?"

He raised an eyebrow. "That puzzles you? All right—I'm biologically forty-four, sixteen years younger than Liesel. Don't bother to count back—I fathered Tregare at fifteen. Liesel chose for genetic reasons, without regard to age. Later she decided I was worth keeping." The tall man looked almost apologetic; then he smiled. "Even among Hulzeins I think I've earned my keep."

"I am sure you have."

Now both brows rose. "Flattery? Or innuendo?"

"No." She shook her head. "Simply the fact that you are here."

The brows returned to normal. "Pardon me; I do persist in underestimating you."

"It is all right. Better that than to expect too much."

"Well. And what else would you like to know?"

She thought. "A personal problem. The man dal Nardo—in his job, he must have a superior. Do you know who it is?"

"If you're thinking of having him *told* to leave you alone, it won't work."

"Of course not. I merely wish to know whether killing him would arouse his department against me also."

"I wouldn't think so. His family's, more likely—but without Stagon I doubt they'd meddle with any Hulzein connection. He's the only bold dal Nardo left; the rest are a ragtag lot.

"Stagon's boss, though—that's Arni Gustafson. I know her mostly by reputation—stubborn but fair-minded. Well, it could do no harm to talk with her."

"Good—I will, then. Now—when I challenge, what weapon is dal Nardo likely to choose? I may as well be practicing."

"But it's *your* choice, Rissa!"

"How can it be, when I am the one making the challenge?"

"On Number One the less formidable antagonist, as judged by their seconds and the officials, has the choice. If the two appear evenly matched, the referee flips a coin to decide."

"Then I will need no specialized practice."

"So? What weapons will you choose?"

"None—except for my body, mind, and training."

"That's insane! Use a gun—anything to keep out of his reach."

"If I am within his reach, he is also within mine. And I think I am faster."

"No, Rissa—he'll kill you."

"Five million Weltmarks say he will not."

"But that's—" He laughed. "I see. If you lose—"

"I have no one to leave it to; it would escheat to your

government. I would prefer that you had some of it instead.''

"And if you win it's a nice profit. Well—I could free that sum easily enough. But I won't do it—I don't *want* to have a stake riding on your death.''

For a moment, tears welled; she blinked them back. "In that case, I may make a will and bequeath you the amount. But if I do so, I shall not tell you.''

THE cloud mass moved on, ceasing to block the sun's heat. Rissa and Hawkman talked of other things—the climate and geography of Number One—its fauna and flora. Rissa asked of local customs; few were greatly different from those of Earth or Far Corner. A memory came. "Hawkman, do you have here a nudity taboo?''

"Not except in the towns, in public. Why?''

"The girl who came to wake me. When I rose from bed bare, she left the room immediately.''

"Oh, that—it's not a taboo, it's status. Yours is the higher; it was improper for her to stay, clothed, when you weren't. She could leave or strip. You were both going downstairs in a few minutes, so she saved herself a little effort—that's all.''

"Good. Because the sun is hot, and I have not felt sunlight on all my skin since I left Earth. Or—is it improper for me to be undressed in your presence?''

"No—or vice versa. But—is this leading up to anything?'' She stiffened; in a moment he gestured as if to erase his words.

She said, slowly, "Hawkman, although I am new here, I realize it could be discourteous to my hostess to try to seduce my host.''

"Rissa, I didn't mean—''

"But of course you did, and the assumption was quite natural. You do not know me yet.''

"You mean there's something in particular, that I don't know?''

"No vows of celibacy or sexual sisterhood—nothing of that

sort. Merely that you do not know my ways or customs, and that with many the invitation to nudity in private *does* imply sex. But from me it does not." Now she laughed. "But do not be crestfallen. I mean no slur on your attractiveness or on my feelings toward you—which are quite . . . warm."

"You embarrass me," he said, not looking at all embarrassed. "Well, then—let's get some sun on us, shall we?"

THEY lay until the sun left the clearing, then repacked the basket and began the downward walk. Where the path was wide enough they walked side by side, hand in hand, swinging the joined arms. At the turn that brought the lodge to sight, they dressed themselves.

"That was pleasant, Hawkman."

"Yes. The family sunbathes occasionally, out of sight of the Lodge, so as not to inconvenience the help. You must join us."

"Thank you." They resumed their walk. He did not take her hand so she took his, firmly. He looked at her but said nothing.

"Hawkman? The duel—could I specify that we fight unclothed?"

"Hmm—I suppose so. What advantage would that give you?"

"Not what you are probably thinking. I would not rely on pain to stop dal Nardo—even made a eunuch, he could still go on and kill me. But the *risk* would make him cautious."

He nodded. "True enough—but you'll need a fighting-hood. If he gets you by the hair, one snap and you're dead. Or will you cut it short?"

"No. I will grease it. If he grasps it, he will make his hands slippery and his grip unsure."

"Have you dueled in this fashion before?"

"No. I thought of the idea while the sun warmed me in the clearing."

He laughed. "You know? I've half a mind to get that five million together after all—and find someone who's fool enough to bet on dal Nardo!"

But she knew that what he said was at least part hyperbole.

INSIDE the Lodge, they parted. Back in her room Rissa mentally reviewed the combat techniques best suited for dealing with vastly larger opponents; shadow-fighting, she practiced those the limited space would allow. She finished with a few calisthenics, then bathed and dressed.

At dinner, Liesel was absent; neither Hawkman nor Sparline offered any explanation. During the meal they spoke little; over coffee, Sparline reported that Tregare had refused to see or speak with her. "Through his spokesman he sent regards to the family, nothing more. Oh—Rissa, I almost forgot —he sent you this note."

Explaining to Hawkman what her message had been, she opened the note and read it aloud. "And the same to you, shipmate."

"Uncommunicative as usual," Hawkman said. "Well, he gets his stubbornness from both sides." His sigh was half a groan. "If only there'd been a way on Earth to get him free and bring him with us. But any attempt would have been his death."

Sparline reached for his hand. "I know that, Hawkman; I knew it then, young as I was. And so does Bran Tregare, by now. It's only that he was embittered for so long—he's struck this pose and held it until it's part of him. Someday, when it wears off—and meanwhile, stop torturing yourself."

"I know. It's only that he's *here*, and won't see us."

"I—" but Rissa thought better of what she would have said—that Tregare might see *her*, and she could plead his family's cause. For she had no right to offer such presumptuous hope.

Hawkman turned to her. "Yes, Rissa?"

"No—it is inconsiderate to intrude my concerns at this time."

"Go ahead," said Sparline. "We could use a new topic."

"The matter of dal Nardo preoccupies me, I am sorry to admit. I think I have made plans as best I can. I started to ask—how soon can I go to the town and begin to implement them?"

Sparline answered. "That's Liesel's decision. I'm sure she'll give you permission when she returns."

"When will that be?"

"We're not sure. Maybe tomorrow, maybe a week. Not long."

Rissa paused. "I do not wish to be ungracious, but why do I need permission? My life—not hers—is at stake."

Sparline looked to Hawkman. He said, "You're here under Liesel's protection. You *can* leave without her sanction, of course—but if you do, you forfeit that protection and further contact with all of us." He made a deprecating gesture. "To you, that may seem foolish—but it is our way. So you must choose."

"Since it is a serious choice, may I think on it for a time?"

"Of course. And I hope you won't be impetuous. I wouldn't like you to be excommunicated from us."

"Nor I," said Sparline.

Rissa said, "*I* certainly would not! Very well; I will try to keep patience." *But not so long that Tregare leaves before I can try to see him . . .*

Sparline brought out drugsticks, but Rissa said, "Not for me, until after the duel. They calm me too much." Sparline looked at Hawkman; he said nothing. She shrugged and put the sticks away.

Servants cleared the table. Hawkman poured liqueurs and said, "Some gaming to relax? Rissa, do you know the game called poker?"

"After a year at Erika's? Of course."

He laughed, opened a thin drawer and brought out cards and chips. "You'll be rusty, I expect, so we'll play for low stakes."

Low, perhaps, thought Rissa, for Hulzein/Morays—most circles would have considered them astronomical. At one point she was down nearly 200,000 Weltmarks, but finished 100,000 ahead. At the end Hawkman told her, "With a little more practice you'll manage well enough."

"I hope so." She yawned. "I have enjoyed this. But if I do not go upstairs soon I shall have to sleep on the table."

The others agreed; companionably they walked up the stairs, then went to their separate rooms. Rissa spent little time preparing for bed, and even less lying awake before sleep.

For Rissa the next days were near to vacuum. Liesel did not return. She saw little of Hawkman or Sparline; young servitors—Castel, Ernol, and others—escorted her as she explored the terrain around the Lodge. She exercised, practiced shadow-fighting and refined her combat plan, ate, read and slept. And one morning she knew she had to decide—the next day, by report, Tregare was leaving.

First things first—she washed and dressed. She sorted her belongings into two groups: the essentials went into her two smaller pieces of luggage; she did not pack the rest.

Slowly and carefully she wrote a brief letter, pausing often to consider the exact meaning of her words. Then she reread it:

Liesel:

I regret leaving without your permission, but I must. I will tell you why; perhaps you can make an exception and forgive me.

Tregare leaves tomorrow; I must see him first—not for myself but because he is too stubborn to meet with any of you. If he will see me I can tell him what he refuses to hear from you. Then perhaps he will agree to see you, also.

It may not be my place to interfere, but I intend to try. Out of gratitude to you—and to Erika, who has been your enemy but never mine. My love to you, and to Hawkman and Sparline. If I survive dal Nardo I hope you will receive me again.

Rissa Kerguelen

She hesitated, then nodded emphatically and sealed the note. Carefully she donned the identity—eyes, nose, fingertips, teeth, the hair in loose, dyed curls—of Tari Obrigo. Leaving the room, she met the girl who had come to wake her.

At breakfast she found Hawkman and Sparline. "Liesel has not returned?"

Sparline shook her head. Hawkman said, "I'm afraid not. Uh—what's your name in the guise you're wearing? And if I may ask, why are you using it?"

"Tari Obrigo. This is how dal Nardo knows me."

"So—you're leaving, after all?"

"Yes, Hawkman." She placed her sealed note on the table. "When Liesel comes back, please give her this. And urge her to read it."

"You've written down your excuses, have you?"

"*Reasons*, Hawkman. Do you recognize no difference?"

"Sometimes. Ah—our meal arrives. Food first, talk later."

"If at all!" Rissa snapped the words out, then regretted them.

Dining was largely silent. Over coffee Rissa said, "May I have the use of an aircar and driver to take me to the city?"

Sparline answered. "Of course, if you're determined to go."

"I am."

"No hesitation?" said Hawkman.

"None."

"Have you thought what this decision means?" said Sparline.

"Of course I have."

"You've waited five days. In two more, Liesel will be back."

"That would be too late."

"For a matter of two days," Hawkman said, "you throw away your connection here and go out to grub it on your own?"

Rissa felt baited. "If—" She caught herself. "Yes."

"Then it's a good thing," said Hawkman, "that Liesel called last night—and granted the permission you would have flouted."

Shaking with rage, she stood. "Why did you not *tell* me?"

"It's well to test a blade," said Sparline, "before trusting it fully."

Suppressing her anger, Rissa sat again. "You are right, of course." Hawkman would have spoken; she waved him to silence. "Now I realize my mistake."

"And what is that?" he said.

"I hoped to spare your damned Hulzein pride. Well, the hell with it—read that note!"

When they had done so, Sparline looked at her and said, "Hawkman kept saying we were underestimating you. He was right."

As much as Rissa wanted to accept the quasi-apology, she could not. "Be that as it may—trust works both ways or neither. Mine is yours for the asking, if you be truthful with me and dispense with games and tests. My distrust, also, is easy enough to manage. Is that last statement clear?"

Hawkman's smile was tentative. "Like crystal. And for my part, I accept your terms. No more games." And Sparline nodded.

Suddenly, her spirits rising, Rissa wanted to seal friendship. "Hawkman—Sparline—perhaps I overreacted. My own tensions are no excuse. Now—you have my loyalty. Do I have yours?"

"On a personal basis, yes," said Hawkman. "You realize, only Liesel speaks for Hulzein Lodge."

But each reached to clasp one of Rissa's hands.

SHE brought the two suitcases; even though not estranged from the Lodge she expected to stay in the town—city?—for a time. Hawkman met her outside, at the aircar.

"Where is the pilot?"

"I'm right here," he said.

"You?"

"To emphasize that you're truly a Hulzein connection. In this way, dal Nardo will see he can't make do with a hired duelist. And such scum won't bother you in my presence."

He took the aircar up at a steep slant, to a calm level of air. She said, "Are you here as male protecting female? I cannot accept that."

He laughed. "Not at all. In fact, Sparline would have brought you, but Liesel's call last night gave her tasks that keep her busy today." Rissa looked at him. Well, if she were to trust him in large matters, she could not question him in smaller ones.

He steered between banks of cloud as though drawn to sunlight. Watching the looming hills and the streams that meandered between them, her thought was that Number One was indeed a world of beauty. Time passed more quickly than she realized; soon, ahead, she saw the spaceport—and beyond it, the settlement.

"Do you recognize *Inconnu*, Hawkman? From outside, I cannot tell the two ships apart. The other was not here when we landed."

"I recognize it. Notice the turret guns, the projectors, topside? Now, *that's* strange—see the clear space around it? I expected he'd still be loading cargo." On his control panel he turned switches. "I don't like this—I'm tuning in on the ship-groundside bands."

They came closer; Rissa saw more details. For a hundred meters around *Inconnu* the ground was empty, and most of those who stood closest were armed. And ship's ramps were up and sealed.

Above the control panel a speaker came to noisy life. The sound was distorted but Rissa recognized Tregare's voice. "You in the aircar—what you think you're trying to pull? Clear off or I'll shoot you down. And *you*, Bleeker—I thought you had better sense. Call off your pipsqueak Air Force—and damned fast!"

Through a different speaker another voice sputtered. Under his breath, Hawkman muttered, "That's Alsen Bleeker." Going no closer, he turned the aircar to circle the ship.

Bleeker's voice came more clearly. "Tregare! It's not mine, that aircar—I swear it isn't! I don't know anything about it—I've been right here, the past six hours since you closed your ship. All I want is my money, you pirate!"

"You got it—exactly as agreed, beforehand."

"I told you, prices went up—it's not my fault."

"Your prices always go up—that's an old groundhog trick. And like it or not, most ships have to pay. But not *Inconnu!*"

"If you want fuel, you'll pay."

Tregare laughed. "I refueled first off; didn't you know? That's an old *spacer* trick. Sign off, Bleeker—I'm done with you." His voice rose. "Now, *you*—the aircar! Who are you? What's your business?"

Rissa whispered "Please!" and took the handset. "Tregare! It is I—Tari Obrigo. I must talk with you."

"Too late, Tari—no time. Bleeker'll be programming the defense missiles on me; I've got to lift. Glad you came, though. See you someday."

"Wait! Your father is here—he brought me."

"Hawkman? Sorry, but for him it's *years* too late—all the years since they left me in that UET hellhole."

She looked to Hawkman, but he said nothing. "They could not help it—they had no choice! And they—they love you— they want to see you!"

"The pirate, the mutineer—in Hulzein Lodge? I doubt it."

Hawkman took the handset. "Bran Tregare, the girl speaks truth. And she thinks enough of you that she would have come here against Liesel's command."

"She's quite a girl, Hawkman. See that you treat her right."

Hawkman's eyebrows rose. Rissa shook her head; he said only, "Yes—but, son, we miss you. Are we ever to see you again?"

When Tregare spoke, his voice was low. "I'll think about it. Next time, maybe."

"And how long until then, Bran? Will your mother live to see that time?"

"I—I hope so." Rissa heard another voice; then Tregare said, briskly now, "Liftoff coming—sixty seconds and counting. Scoot that car hard and fast, Hawkman—this lift is going to make waves—not like the time with you, Tari." Hawkman turned the car and accelerated toward the town. They heard Tregare, faintly, speaking to someone else. Then, after a pause, "Good-bye, Hawkman—Tari. And the message I sent the family—make that *warm* regards.''

"Not—not love?" she said.

"In person, maybe—we'll see. Tregare out." And the ship lifted.

Tregare had not exaggerated. Looking back Rissa saw people, lying flat for safety, rolled along the ground by the great blast. The ship still aground rocked and almost fell. When the shock wave reached the aircar they felt a mighty buffet, and Hawkman was busy fighting the controls. Then *Inconnu* was gone and the air quieted.

"Thanks for trying, Rissa. If it hadn't been for that blood-sucking Bleeker, maybe . . ." Then he smiled. "Well, at least the boy spoke to me."

"Yes." But her thought was elsewhere. "Hawkman? Now we know more about Tregare's reputation, do we not? Hè is called 'pirate' because he refuses to be made victim."

"Eh? Oh, yes—we'd suspected that much, knowing what some traders do to ships that can't fight. The Hulzeins, by the way, don't follow that practice—we charge what the market will bear, but once agreed, the price is firm." After a succession of turns that mystified Rissa, Hawkman descended beside a large green building and landed. He turned to her. "You may have stirred up local politics a bit today. I expected it, as soon as I saw you'd have no chance for private speech with Bran Tregare—and you'll notice I didn't try to stop you from saying what you did."

"I do not know what you mean, Hawkman."

"It's only that until now no one on this planet—outside the Lodge—knew that Tregare is a Hulzein." He laughed. "But don't worry about it—we've had storms before. We weather them."

INSIDE the building, an elevator took them to the top floor. The office they entered occupied a full quarter of that floor; its large windows faced the Big Hills on one side and the town on the other. The plain, tinted metal walls were hung with pictures of varied scenic views. Behind a desk, a tall, heavily built woman stood to meet them.

"Hawkman Moray." She shook his hand and turned to take Rissa's. "I'm Arni Gustafson."

"Tari Obrigo."

The woman frowned. Rissa eyed her—squarish face, thick brown hair cut in a full bang to the eyebrows, then straight around below the ears. Finally; "Oh yes—*that* one. Hawkman? Are you here to claim Hulzein protection for her, against dal Nardo?"

"Not by blood or marriage, but she is a connection. However, I merely brought her here to speak with you."

"I see. Her status means he can't hire her death without Hulzein retaliation. I'll tell him."

She spoke again to Rissa. "How in this world did you manage to begin your stay here by rousing Stagon's blood-thirst? I'd have guessed you more apt to rouse him in other ways."

"He made stupid threats; instead of cowering, I returned his fire in kind. Nothing more—except that others were present and saw."

The woman sat again, gesturing toward a chair. Rissa seated herself; Hawkman moved to do so but Arni Gustafson said, "Your pardon, Hawkman—would you please wait in the lounge across the way? I'd like to speak with her alone." Her hand moved at her desk console; at the upper end of hearing range Rissa heard a thin hum. Hawkman, at the door, turned with a worried look. Rissa smiled and nodded to him, and he left.

She knew that hum; Erika had also used truth fields. The ultrasonic waves that scanned her would report her reactions on the console.

She would, she thought, have to be very careful what she said.

"Have you come," said Gustafson, "because I'm in authority over dal Nardo? If so, it's a waste of time. I have no say-so in his private life; I can't stop him from killing you."

"I knew that. My question is this—when I kill him, will there be any retaliation from your agency?"

"When?" The woman stared at the console, looked puzzled and shook her head. "You mean that, don't you?" Rissa kept silent. "Yes, you do, all right. Well, then—the answer's no. I don't want Stagon killed—I don't like him, but he's capable, and about as honest as the next. If he dies, I'll be briefly inconvenienced. But *how* he dies—as with how he lives—is none of my business."

"Good. Thank you, Ms. Gustafson. That is all I need to know."

"Wait—sit back down—*I* want to know a few things. First —what is zombie gas?"

"I—I have never seen it used." *So far, so good.* "From the name, I assume it would render the victim subject to the will of another, without the normal ego defenses."

"And you're immunized against it?"

"It cannot harm me."

"You intended to use it on dal Nardo?"

"I intended to do whatever was needed to escape his threats."

"Young woman, I don't like the idea of you running around in my jurisdiction with something like that. Where do you carry the stuff—in a pocket? A piece of jewelry?"

"I cannot show you." Sensing annoyance, Rissa added, "I mean, I have none with me. On a world where no one is immunized, it seems to me that it would be irresponsible to use such a thing—except in extreme emergency."

The older woman scowled at her console and shook her head. "There's something," she muttered, "but it's not clear." She looked up. "You've breached no law—yet—so I can't slip you a babble pill to get at whatever you're talking your way around. So I'll try it another way. What's your attitude toward dal Nardo? And does it include anyone else?"

"Dal Nardo intends me dead. Now it seems he must do it himself. My only alternative, I am told, is to kill him instead—so if I must, I must. As to others, I mean no harm to any who mean none to me." After a moment, she smiled. "Is that good enough?"

"Better than most. All right—I guess you pass. I must say, your attitudes don't fit dal Nardo's description."

"You did not try to treat me as he did."

"No—he's one of a kind. Let me give you some advice. If you went and apologized to him, he might—just *might*—settle for first blood or first mutilation rather than death. If he doesn't, you haven't lost anything."

Rissa shook her head. "I would lose something very important to me. But I will give *him* the chance to apologize, if he wishes."

"Tari Obrigo, you're a hopeless case! Well, I'm glad to have met you, and truly sorry it's probably the last time."

"Thank you—but I expect you *will* see me again, after all."

UNTIL they left the building, Hawkman said nothing. Then; "Any problems?"

"Not really. Dal Nardo's death is his own business. And I hear well at the high end of the range—I knew when she turned the truth field on. Then I needed to plan quite carefully each word I said."

"I had the hunch that you're hiding something—but for the life of me I can't guess it. Well, I won't pry."

"I—it is only that—" Then in a burst of frankness she told him of her impromptu invention and dal Nardo's reaction. "But if his aides have spread the story, you see? It might be useful another time."

He laughed. "It might, at that. Well—do you want to see dal Nardo now, or have some lunch first?"

"I could not eat. I confess—my stomach is tight within me. Let it be dal Nardo."

"I don't blame you. All right, it's a short hop—or would you rather walk? You can see the building from here." He pointed; she recognized it.

"Let us walk. The exercise will loosen my nerves and muscles."

THEY walked into the Provost's office without knocking or

announcement. Hawkman said, "You know me, dal Nardo. You also know Tari Obrigo. I'm here to inform you that she is a Hulzein connection, though not of blood or marriage—so you can't set a hired duelist on her without answering for it. That's my message; from now on I merely observe the formalities."

Dal Nardo's heavy cheeks flushed; he drew breath, but as the cold lump at Rissa's stomach dissolved into heat, she spoke. "Since Hawkman is not immunized, you may feel free today to threaten me all you like. But there is no need for threats. I have an offer for you—and if you refuse it, another."

"If you offer to lie down, be buried, and let me plant frost grain over you, I accept. But don't think to placate me with an apology."

"I had no such thought. My first offer is to accept an apology from *you*—a courteous one, judged suitable by Hawkman Moray—and leave here and disturb you no further."

The man shook his head and smiled broadly. "I'm fascinated; I've never heard such long-winded fertilizer."

"Well. So much for that one. My second offer is this: I challenge you."

"You challenge *me*? Ah, I see—for first blood or some such trifle, to avoid my own challenge. A silly trick—I refuse it."

"You mistake me, dal Nardo. I challenge to the death, unless you make plea for lesser terms."

Again he shook his head. "There is some deception here."

Hawkman spoke. "There's none. I'm here to see to that."

"This girl challenges me to the death? You say that, Moray?"

"*She* says it. Talk to her, not to me."

"Then I accept—I accept! And if you think you have some advantage with a new weapon, let me tell you that only weapons familiar to this world are allowed." He shrugged. "As for me, I prefer to use none at all."

"That is good," said Rissa. "For that is my choice also."

"You *want* to die—I knew you must be crazy, to insult me in my own place."

"Stay with business; I am not yet done."

"Ah, I see it—you'll specify protective suits. They won't—"

"No, dal Nardo—we will fight nude. No weapons, no suits —only ourselves."

His eyes narrowed. "It won't work, what you're thinking."

She laughed. "If you knew what I am thinking, you would make the apology I asked."

"Oh, no—you don't have—never mind. When do we meet?"

"Our seconds decide that, I believe. Hawkman—will you represent me and help choose suitable officals?" He nodded. "Then name your own seconds, dal Nardo; have them call Hawkman and arrange terms." She looked into the man's eyes; his gaze was equally fixed upon her. "All right," she said. "We are finished here; I will next see you when and where it is agreed." She turned away. "Shall we go, Hawkman?"

"Good-bye, fertilizer," said Stagon dal Nardo.

She looked around and said, "It is well for the planet's soil that you are so much larger than I."

The door closing behind them muffled dal Nardo's retort. Rissa took Hawkman's arm and said, "You mentioned lunch? I have truly worked up an appetite!"

THE restaurant was high-ceilinged and drafty. "The food's plain here," said Hawkman, "but good. Or it had better be—we own the place."

Rissa smiled. "After eleven years of Welfare food, I am hardly a gourmet. Even Erika could not train my tastes so quickly. If food is fresh and flavorful, I like it."

Hawkman ordered for them; she did not recognize his choices by name, but when the food arrived, its tastes lived up to its aromas. She fed until sated and still could not clean her platter.

"It *was* good, Hawkman."

He grinned. "The way you picked at your food, I'd never

have guessed." Then, sobering; "About dal Nardo—are you sure you know what you're doing?"

"I am building a plan into my mind so that I will perform it mechanically. It is flexible, with alternatives for moves that fail. More than that I cannot do. But I think my plan will suffice."

"But he's so damned powerful! And faster than you'd think."

"Let my adrenaline subside, Hawkman—it serves no purpose now and might hamper digestion of this excellent meal. But I will say this—on Earth, combat techniques have improved from what dal Nardo could have been taught here. How many years' advantage I have of him in that way, I cannot know—but there will be some. Also, for physical combat, he would do well to carry less belly."

"Don't count on—no, you're right—let's change the subject." He poured wine and told her of the city. "Population's well into six figures—nearly a fifth of the planet's total. Do you know why it's called One Point One? I guess you'd have to have been here."

She thought. "No—I see it—the planet, Number One. The town, One Point One. Named, after all, by officers of Escaped Ships—with mathematical orientation and, it seems, a sense of humor."

"I wish more of that humor survived among the colonists."

She moved the glass in her hands, swirling the wine gently and watching the light it refracted. "Yes—your world is as much cutthroat as Earth, in some aspects. Are we humans good for no other way?"

"I don't know; competition seems to be our middle name. That's not all bad—but we don't seem to know where to stop. Well, what more would you like to know about our city?"

From the air, she had noticed that One Point One was loosely patterned, with areas of open ground scattered throughout. Now she learned that here was the planet's only major star base, the one port capable of fully servicing interstellar ships. "So that's why Hulzein Lodge is where it is," said Hawkman. "Quite a distance from our major landholdings. And—"

She waved a hand. "Thank you, Hawkman—but I am as filled with facts as with food—and need time to digest both."

"All right. Let's go—we'll take your gear to where you'll be staying."

THE sign on the squat beige building read "Maison Renalle." Hawkman said, "It's not tops for luxury, but it's secure: The guard system's unobtrusive but effective. And the only bugged rooms—except for security monitor—are the ones Liesel's arranged specially, to plant suspicious characters in."

"Thank you for the warning. I will be most discreet."

"You? But—" Then he saw she was laughing, silently. "Your character is not merely suspicious, Rissa—sometimes, as now, it's downright disreputable.

"No—" He waved a hand. "I challenge you—to lunch again, next time I'm in town."

Now she laughed aloud. "Hawkman, you are good for me." She turned to him. "You are like—well, younger than my father whom I lost, and older than my brother who was destroyed—but somehow both of them. I am very glad to have come to know you."

He would have spoken but she shook her head. "Let us go in now."

HER room, not large, had an air of comfort—and even more, of safety. Her window, facing the Big Hills, looked thick enough to stop bullets. And she knew that the slanted metal flecks within it, that slightly hazed her view, would briefly diffuse a laser beam. The door, though it moved easily, was massive; the room's facilities were self-contained. Knowing Hulzein thoroughness, she trusted the thickness and composition of the walls.

"Notice the viewscreen terminal?" Hawkman said. "The

red-in-blue button gives direct communication to the Lodge. On scramble; it can't be tapped."

"Very nice—I have never seen such a safety vault."

"We try to take care of our own."

"Do you really think I need such precautions?"

"Maybe not—but it's here, so why not use it? At the least, it will impress a few people."

"All right—but after dal Nardo, I think I would prefer less fortified quarters." She smiled. "Now bend down and let me kiss you thanks, and you can go home and forget all about me."

They kissed; then he left her to herself.

AFTER unpacking, she sat to reread some of her notes from the time at Erika's, and to add to those she had made since her arrival. Her comment to Hawkman had been accurate, she decided—some forms and customs differed, but in essentials Number One's power system resembled Earth's. It was newer and less rigid, yes—but from her viewpoint the only important difference was that part of it was on *her* side. Or, she added mentally, probationally so . . .

She watched twilight engulf the Hills and called to place her order for dinner. "A light meal," she said. "For the meat, two grilled slices of loin from the—what is the word?—female bushstomper, at any rate. Leave it juicy, please. For the rest—a small plate of fruits and fresh vegetables—whatever kinds you recommend. And a bottle of upland red wine, please."

She ate in dimming light and sipped wine until light and wine were gone. Then she turned a switch to brighten the room and wondered what to do with her evening. She switched the viewscreen to an entertainment channel, setting the alarm to notify her of incoming calls.

For a few minutes she watched a sports event—two manned captive kites in contest. The object was to down the other, kite and all. It looked dangerous, but somehow the loser caught air at the last instant and landed unhurt—or, at worst, bruised.

Then, after a series of announcements, some political and some commercial, came a drama. The characters did not interest her much, but a world's dramatic values can reflect its attitudes, so she watched and listened closely.

A middle-aged woman spent much time bemoaning the loss of her brother, gone to space. Her husband lost patience with her; now and then she took lovers, younger men. One evening she made overtures to a young spaceman; slightly drunk, he rejected and insulted her, so she challenged him and killed him in a duel. Rissa had guessed the ending—who could he be but the long-lost brother? She snorted—surely *she* could write better stories. Then she thought again: could she write to suit the tastes of this world? Probably not.

She reset the viewscreen to its normal communications function and sat brooding. She had not liked the story, but it nagged at her—what was important about it? What was its real theme? Not the foolish woman, not the trite coincidence—finally she had it. "The long view—of course! On Earth it touches very few, but here—" Yes—on Number One it would be a fact of life, a preoccupation.

By her standards the hour was not late, but with the puzzle solved, she decided to go to bed. For a time she lay awake, belatedly tense and anxious. Dal Nardo *was* formidable—had she pushed her luck too far this time? Life was sweet . . .

Finally she visualized the man as standing in one small compartment of her mind. She closed that compartment firmly. Then she relaxed and slept.

SHE lay abed until nearly mid-morning, then spent considerable time in bathing, grooming, and eating breakfast. Finally she could no longer avoid the problem—what was she going to do with herself all this day? She voiced her thoughts aloud. ". . . not supposed to go out, probably—but he did not *say* . . ." "Change identities? And probably compromise another one, if any watched Tari come in and—say—Lysse go out." Abruptly she stood. "Oh, the hell with it. Why should I give them satisfaction by hiding?" She set the screen to record incoming calls and herself recorded a brief greeting for possible callers.

Looking out, she judged the morning to be cool, and put on a jacket. She went out by the main entrance—attempting no evasive, inconspicuous exit—into sunlight and clear, brisk air. Looking about, she decided to walk toward the city's central part.

In roughly fifteen minutes she reached a district of narrow streets and small shops. Here, walkways were unpaved—night rain had left mud and puddles. As she picked her way through a treacherous patch, someone bumped her from behind. Barely, she kept her balance—but heard a splash and a cry, and turned to see a brightly dressed young man flat in the mud.

"Oh, I *am* sorry—it is so slippery!" She bent to help him.

"No, you don't—not again! Keep your hands to yourself." Slowly he got his feet under him and stood. She saw that he was tall and slim, near his biological mid-twenties. "Now, then," he said. "Your name?"

"Tari Obrigo—and I really am sorry—I did not see you."

When she spoke the name, he nodded, and she knew. *This one is not much of an actor*. He said, "Not likely you didn't. You tripped me, as an insult—to ruin my clothes and make me look foolish. Well, we'll see about that. I don't—"

"Who *are* you, by the way?"

"Blaise Tendal—and for what you did, I challenge you. No limit."

His clothes were bright enough, but cheaply made. "A moment, first—let us clarify the matter of status. Are you sure you are eligible? I am Hulzein-connected."

Impatiently he nodded. "*I* know who you are. I—"

"Then why did you ask?"

"Well—there's the formalities, you know."

"You still have not told me your status, Blaise Tendal."

"In a minute." He waved her words away. "Is your connection by blood? By marriage?"

"Neither—and you knew that, as well."

"That's right. So I'm eligible. My wife's a dal Nardo. Good enough?"

Smiling, she nodded. "Quite suitable. But still I am afraid I cannot oblige you."

"The hell you can't! If you don't know the rules, here they are—you meet me or get down on your knees in the mud and apologize. Otherwise I'll whip you through the streets. What do you say *now*, Obrigo?"

"That you have overlooked a superseding rule. Previous challenges must be honored before new ones may be made. You will have to wait your turn, Tendal. I am committed to meet someone else first."

"I don't believe you! Who?"

"Who but Stagon dal Nardo?"

Tendal's face went vacant. "He didn't tell me—now I've gone and ruined my clothes for nothing."

Rissa laughed. "Oh? Moments ago you said it was *I* who did it."

"Well, you did!" He scowled at her, then grinned. "So he caught up with you after all! I'd like to've seen you when he challenged you."

"I wish you had—for it was I who challenged." He said nothing but his look was skeptical. She said, "Tell me—how much was he to pay you?"

"I—oh, swallow your tongue!" He made as if to spit at her, then turned abruptly to leave. On the slick mud he slipped and nearly fell again—only by flapping like an awkward bird did he keep his footing. He paused to look back and glare, for she was laughing helplessly. Then he walked away, striding stiffly, placing his feet with care.

Rissa wiped her eyes and shrugged. Was this the peril from which she must be guarded?

SHE resumed her walk and came to a section of food-serving stalls. The spicy aroma of one tidbit—chopped meat wrapped in thin dough, deep-fried and served on a stick—aroused her appetite. But breakfast was too recent, and when she looked more closely the cleanliness of the place did not impress her, so she walked on.

YOUNG RISSA

The sun was well past zenith when she turned back toward Maison Renalle, and lower when she reached it. She went to her room; before checking on possible calls, she ordered food. She tried to describe the things she had seen. ". . . on a stick, yes. Do you make them here?"

"We can, certainly. How many would you like?"

"Of the size they serve at the market stalls? Three, I think. If it would not be too much trouble." The other's gesture said it would not. "And a little of . . ." She ordered bits and pieces, as for a picnic. "And—no, nothing more. That will do, thank you."

She opened a flask of brandy and poured half-full its ornate cap that doubled as a glass. Sipping, she set the screen to replay any calls that might have come in.

The first was an elderly man—quite bald, with a thin, bony face and gray goatee. "My name's Bleeker, Ms. Obrigo— Alsen Bleeker. I've got to talk to you, about the pirate—I mean spaceman—Captain Tregare. It's urgent; I must see you before—while you're still—very soon. I'm in my office every day; anyone can tell you where it is—" and he gave the address, which meant nothing to Rissa. "Call me as soon as you view this. Please!" She thought; *The old fool has the tact of a sledgehammer, making it so obvious he expects dal Nardo to kill me!*

Next were two commercial calls of the kind she supposed were made routinely to all new residents. One wished to rent her a ground or aircar; the other offered a tour of the Slab Jumbles area, at the southern end of the first range of Big Hills. On second estimate, she decided those bids might not be so routine, after all. In strange vehicles and wild countryside, accidents can happen. Dal Nardo wished her dead—perhaps any means would do. Since she was not interested in either offer, just yet, she shrugged and filed the ideas for future consideration.

Her meal arrived; she sat and nibbled on one of the somethings-on-a-stick—it *was* delicious. Then she pushed the button again.

Hawkman's displeased face appeared on the screen. "You *are* foolish, to go out at this time. Well, no point in scolding

—if you're seeing this you'll scoff at caution, and if—well, either way I'm wasting breath.

"At any rate, assuming your luck's holding, call me as soon as you can. I'll be available all evening." The screen blanked.

Quickly, as she ate, she sampled the remaining messages. Each was a commercial inquiry; as soon as she determined that, she punched on to the next and was done with the lot in less than a minute. Then she punched the red-in-blue button.

The girl who answered was one who had escorted Rissa on a walk near the Lodge, but Rissa could not recall her name, so she smiled and said, "It is pleasant to see you again. May I speak with Hawkman Moray, please?"

She waited briefly and Hawkman appeared. "I am sorry if you worried," she said, "but as you see, I am unharmed." Before he could answer, she told him of her brush with Tendal. "If he is a sample of the quality of dal Nardo's paid killers—"

"Hold on, there." Hawkman frowned. "Blaise Tendal may have appeared clumsy, but he's not. He fights with or without weapons and has more kills than any hired duelist living—except one, and she's retired. Tendal's socially inept, yes—he's not intelligent and in some ways he's not sane. He especially hates women—he's impotent with them. You're lucky he didn't forget all rules and attack when you laughed at him."

"But he said he is married—and to a dal Nardo."

"Yes? Wait—I'll check the public records, on the computer channel." She saw his upper arm move, but his hand was off-screen. After a time, he said, "The marriage was registered the day you arrived here—dal Nardo wasted no time making sure his pet killer would have status to match you."

"But at that time he did not know my exact status."

"Making *sure*, I said. Now let me show you how far the man will go. Tendal's married to Stagon's own daughter, who is still a season or two short of puberty."

"Is that sort of thing legal here?"

"So long as the bride stays home and the marriage isn't consummated until suitable, it's legal enough. But here's how it would have worked, Rissa, in dal Nardo's planning. After Tendal killed you, the marriage would be annulled and Tendal would be paid a settlement for his consent—*not* a hired duelist's fee for killing Stagon's enemy.

"Do you begin to understand what you're faced with here?"

"Oh, yes, Hawkman." She smiled. "It is so much like Earth that I feel right at home."

He could not hold his laughter, but then he sobered. "Almost, your confidence makes me feel it with you. But logic tells me—Rissa, perhaps you should reconsider—return to the Lodge, wait for the next ship and leave on it. Or change identities again and start over, here. Life is such a fragile thing, and dal Nardo is anything but fragile." Eye to eye, he looked at her. "Don't you understand? The more I think on it, the more I fear you'll be killed."

A shudder racked her. "I know, Hawkman. I have to fight that thought myself, or else it might make itself true. So do not reinforce it, please. Because there are no choices—I have pledged to meet dal Nardo and there is no way I could bring myself to break that pledge. Now tell me—is there word yet of the time and place for that meeting?"

He shook his head. "Not yet—his second hasn't called me. Perhaps because he hoped Blaise Tendal would act first. And —yes, I knew you wouldn't renege on your challenge—but I couldn't help suggesting it. Rissa—at the least, won't you come back here and consider alternate plans?"

"Yes—and no. I will return, because the boredom of one room is too much for me and because it is unkind to cause you worry by going out. But my plans are firm—and at the Lodge I can practice them more efficiently."

She made a grimace. "It was a mistake, Hawkman, for me to take residence in One Point One so soon."

SHORTLY before sunset, Sparline brought the aircar. As they took Rissa's luggage aboard and the flight began, the tall woman said little. After two attempts at conversation, Rissa said, "Have I displeased you? I had no such intent."

After a look ahead, Sparline turned to her. "No. I'm concerned, partly about you and partly—oh, I don't know."

Rissa looked at her. With her hair parted and worn in two coils covering the ears, the contours of her face were changed —not softened, exactly, but emphasized differently. "Even without disguises, Sparline, you seldom look the same. It is an enviable trait." Then; "I appreciate your concern, but do not let it tax you, for that would weigh on me also and lessen my chances. But—what else disturbs you?"

Sparline looked ahead again and changed course slightly. "I've been riding myself with spurs—drawing blood from my own flanks, you might say—for the way we dawdled, testing you. If we hadn't, you might have reached Bran Tregare in time."

"No! The ship had been closed for hours. Tregare could not have opened it without a battle with Bleeker's men." Bleeker! She'd forgotten to tell Hawkman . . .

"You know that for sure?" Rissa nodded. "Well, then—I guess I can quit blaming myself. So—tell me about dal Nardo —and Blaise Tendal. Hawkman's not much of a reporter."

The telling, interrupted by many questions, whiled away the rest of the flight.

HER room was the same; someone had neatly stowed the things she had left behind. She bathed and changed and was brushing her hair when the dinner summons came. The Tari Obrigo curls looked a bit limp, she thought, so she tied them back at her nape and went downstairs.

Liesel and Sparline were at the table, set for four, with wine before them but no food as yet. Liesel waved Rissa to a chair and reached to touch her hand. "I've heard of your adventures; I'm pleased you survived them. Have some wine. Hawkman's delayed—some kind of skywatch alert—we won't wait."

"Thank you." Rissa sat. "I hope your own business was successful?"

"Adequate. Fennerabilis is nicely stalemated at the Windy Lakes." She paused. "Hawkman also told how you tried to reach Bran Tregare. Pride says our problems are none of your business—but pride be damned! I'm grateful to you for trying."

Rissa felt a rush of warmth for the older woman. "I am sorry I left it so late, but I was told—I did not want to estrange myself, so I waited until the last. And when Tregare had to seal the ship—it happened during the previous night."

Liesel shook her head. "I should have kept in touch; I usually do. But things got—snicky, the young folks call it—and I was too busy to check on what I thought was a stable situation here." She laughed, but her face did not show laughter. "I'm no good at delegating authority—even to Hawkman or Sparline, who use it every bit as well as I do." Now she relaxed visibly. "All right—have you met any other interesting people, besides dal Nardo and Gustafson and that freak Blaise Tendal, who kills because he can't bed a woman honestly?"

"In a way. There was a call recorded—I forgot to tell Hawkman—from the old man Alsen Bleeker, the one who caused Tregare to seal ship early." As nearly as she could recall it, she repeated the message. "For myself, I have no reason to call him. But if you think it might be useful, I will do so."

Two boys entered with a serving cart and began to distribute its contents. "Don't serve Mr. Moray's place yet," said Liesel. "Leave the cart; his food will stay hot." Then, to one boy, "Carlin, when you're done with this, fetch a communicator terminal, please." The boy nodded. Liesel said, "Rissa, I think you'd better see what the man has to say. Aside from the normal push-and-take, we've had no quarrel with him—now maybe we do. This snick with *Inconnu* shows that we and the ships waste too much effort trying to suck each others' blood—effort we should save for when we need it against UET." She sighed. "It's too bad it took so long, and a personal grievance at that, to convince me."

Rissa waited until the boys left; she saw that Liesel was talking over their heads, but unsure of the lines here between open

and secret information, felt she had best not try to do the
same. Then she said, "You will want me to accept information
but not give it. Correct?" Liesel nodded. "And shall I ask
questions, or is it too likely I would ask the wrong things?"

"Eat up," said Liesel, "and let me think, while *I'm*
eating." After a time she opened a drawer and brought out a
writing tablet and stylus. "You—only—will be on the screen.
The wall behind you is featureless; it won't tell him anything.
Give no sign that you're not alone. If I shake my head, you're
on the wrong track—stop right there. And I can coach you
some with written questions and answers—the cue words, I
mean—I'm sure you improvise well on short notice."

" 'Play it by ear,' is how my mother said it. Or, think on
your feet—though I shall be sitting."

Sparline laughed. "She'll do, Liesel. And—leave her as free
to respond, as you can. Don't try to keep too tight a rein."

Liesel, mouth full, waved a hand. After a moment; "*I* know
that. Now, for the love of peace, let's eat!"

Conversation lagged. The boy Carlin brought the viewscreen and, at Liesel's direction, set it before Rissa and slightly
to one side, partially covering Hawkman's unused place.
When they were down to coffee and liqueurs, Liesel said, "All
right, Rissa—it's time. Do you remember the number?"

"Yes, but it is for his office."

"That'll do; the call will relay to his residence. If that
doesn't work we can try some contingent numbers."

"All right." Rissa punched for Bleeker's office. The screen
stayed dark; a voice said, "Automatic, speaking. This terminal is not occupied. Relay will connect you to an alternate
terminal. Please wait." Perhaps ten seconds passed; the screen
flickered, went dark, then lit. A plump face appeared, that of
a man or woman wearing a tight hood that covered the scalp,
ears, and most of the forehead. The voice sounded like a
woman's.

"Who is calling, and who do you want here?"

Liesel shook her head; Rissa guessed her meaning. "I am
calling at Alsen Bleeker's request. Is he available?"

"I must know who is calling."

"I would like *your* name, please."

"Lennis Betorin. And yours?"

"When I eventually reach Alsen Bleeker, I will tell him that Lennis Betorin prevented my reaching him earlier—unless you would like to forget your protocol and connect us immediately."

"I—yes, of course." The face moved away; Rissa saw part of a room, the focus too poor to make out details. Liesel grinned broadly and reached to pat Rissa's hand.

They waited until Bleeker's gaunt face showed on the screen. "Ms. Obrigo! Well, it took you long enough. I—"

"I called as soon as you reached the top of my priority list. Now, then—what is it you wish to tell me?"

"Tell you? No, I—"

"I assumed you had important information for me. If not, I must get on with other matters. I am sure you understand."

"Wait! Can't you talk a minute? I'll make it worth your while."

"How much?"

Bleeker's thin lips stretched over long yellow teeth. "Well, now—how much are you asking?"

"It depends—do you mean Weltmarks or deaths?"

"*Deaths!* What are you talking about?"

Rissa shrugged. "Money is one currency, death another. Those who wield power usually deal in both. I am merely curious as to your rate of exchange."

"Don't talk such foolishness—not on a public circuit."

"This end is not public—nor, I think, is yours." She waited.

His breath, drawn between clenched teeth, made a whistling sound. "Dal Nardo?" He shook his head; sparse wisps of hair moved on his scalp. "You can't know enough to make *that* job worth it."

"Nor do I ask it. What made you think I do?"

"But everybody knows—I mean, surely it's obvious—"

"Not in my case, Bleeker." She deliberately omitted the honorific and saw Liesel's approving nod. "But we waste time. You said you want to talk. I am waiting."

He leaned closer; she saw blue veins pulse at his temples. "Obrigo—from where you are, can you speak safely?"

"I am quite safe. And you?"

"I mean the Hulzeins—I know you're connected. And I have to ask you some things about them—in strictest confidence. Do I have your word?"

"I shall not repeat anything you say to me about them." Sparline put hands to mouth, muffling laughter. Liesel smiled briefly, then frowned at Sparline and shook her head.

Bleeker's knuckle rubbed his nose. "It's about Tregare—I swear *I* didn't know he was Hulzein until you and Moray announced it on open frequencies—or I'd have kept to groundside ways, dealing with him. As it was—well, the ships run rich; we have to take what we can. You understand?" He coughed. "Ah—a younger like you—what *can* you understand?"

"I understand you made agreement and then changed price—and that Tregare would not be gouged. An unfortunate dispute, that one."

"Yes, yes—that's what I mean. Ms. Obrigo—Tari, isn't it? —are you in touch with the Hulzeins? I can't reach them— they won't talk to me. Do you know if they plan . . . retaliation?" Then; "Just tell me anything you can—I'll pay you well."

Rissa did not look to Liesel. She paused, then said, "I can give you no evaluation, overall. I will share a few facts—put them together for yourself, however they may fit. And I agree —you *will* pay me well, if only for my silence. Well, then—

"One: I came to this planet on *Inconnu.* I have some acquaintance with Tregare, and I am not his enemy.

"Two: From what you overheard, you know something of Tregare's relations with the Hulzeins. Rightly or not, you may have deduced more.

"Three: I would not have you think that Hawkman Moray is pleased with your role in *Inconnu*'s early departure. But if he plans to make his displeasure tangible, he did not tell me.

"Four: If you wish me to act as your go-between with the Hulzeins, I will do so—for a price, of course."

Bleeker made a face as though tasting something foul. "You? What can you do? You're good with words, Obrigo, but dal Nardo—he'll have you dead before you could be of real use to me. Well—I suppose it was worth the try."

He moved a hand and started to turn away. "One moment, Bleeker!" The hand stopped; again he looked at her. "You spoke of payment; we are not done with that. For what I have told you, and for my silence—" She smiled. "—a half million, I would say. Is tomorrow convenient—or the next day, perhaps?"

Rage bulged the old man's eyes and colored his sallow cheeks, but reluctantly he nodded. "Come to my office—I'll pay you there."

"I will come. Since I do not know its location, I am sure Hawkman Moray will assign me a suitable escort." *So you need not bother to set up any cheap dal Nardo ambushes . . .*

Bleeker swallowed. "I'll expect you. Now, if that's all—"

Laughter escaped her, a brief burst that caught her off guard. "No—one more thing. You seem convinced dal Nardo will kill me. Is your conviction worth five million to you?"

The man frowned. "You'd bet on your own death?"

"On my life, rather—five million, even money. Will you risk it—money—where I risk my life?"

"You have that much?"

"And more. I—" Liesel waved a sheet of paper. Rissa scanned it and said, "And of course the Hulzeins stand behind any wager I make." Liesel spread the fingers of both hands. Ten? All right. Including her own five, or added to it? Assume the latter. "And with that in mind, perhaps you would like to make it fifteen?"

The man's eyes narrowed. "Gambling isn't my habit—"

"Of course, if you have not the courage . . ."

"I'll take ten! If the bet's bonded."

"Surely." She moved a switch. "My terminal is set to record—set yours also, and we will repeat the terms."

Bleeker's nod was hesitant, but moments later the wager was duly recorded, and Rissa said, "That is all now, I think. Good night." She cut the circuit and looked to Liesel.

The older woman touched Rissa's hand with one finger. "A few times you ignored my cues, but overall I couldn't have done it better myself. Ten million, old tight-gut Bleeker bet! You took me right on that one; I hoped you could get him to fifteen. Now he's got a fresh worry to distract him. Yes, Rissa—you did well."

Sparline said, "The best is that he's left hanging from his own kite, needing to learn if we're out to gut him. He'll be in touch again, Rissa. And then—"

Liesel's palm slapped the table. "He'll call Maison Renalle!" She turned the communicator to her and punched buttons. "There. Now his call gets relayed here, but he won't know it. Rissa, you'd better have this terminal in your room, and facing a blank wall."

"Yes," said Rissa. "A moment." She adjusted switches and, as she had done in the city, recorded an answer for incoming calls. "I will leave it set to record from now on." Then she said, "I wonder what is keeping Hawkman. He must be very hungry."

"He'll have eaten," Liesel said. "Some snack or other. I doubt he'd join us here this late, unless he looks elsewhere when he comes in, and can't find us."

Sparline said, "Liesel—what's next for Bleeker? When he calls again?"

"Hadn't thought much, yet—give him more string, first, and see if lack of wind brings him down by itself, before we need to act. But I *will* think on it—possibly, here's our chance to catch him between more worries than he can manage and absorb his holdings, or at least get voting control."

"Then your bet on my life is merely to harass Bleeker?"

"Rissa—" Liesel shook her head. "Didn't Erika teach you? *Every* move serves as many uses as possible. And by the way—I assume we're splitting the bet down the middle, you and I?"

"If you like—I do not care. If you prefer, I will take it all."

Liesel stood, moved to Rissa, and held the girl's head against her bosom. "There, now—I've chilled you, haven't I?—mixing cold business with the hot risk of your very blood. Didn't mean to—but that's how we are, looking for every advantage, always. But believe me—we do value your life."

Before Rissa could answer, Liesel moved away. "I'm tired; good night." She left, and Sparline smiled at Rissa, then followed. Rissa drained her wine and went to her own bed.

YOUNG RISSA

• • •

NEXT morning she woke early and rose at once. Dressed and briefly groomed, downstairs she found no one in the dining room or the room where she and Sparline had breakfasted. She followed the sound of voices to the kitchen. Inside were two cooks and several young servitors and other retainers. At her entrance, the talk ceased.

She smiled. "Please—you must not allow me to interrupt you." The buzz of conversation resumed. She turned to the older cook—a fattish woman, gray-haired and red-cheeked. "Out there—" She motioned with her head. "I found no one to breakfast with. I wonder if I might have a snack here."

"Sure, Ms. Obrigo—sit where you please."

In a corner, without his habitual hood and glasses, Castel sipped coffee. Her guess had been right; he was albino. She went to his small table. "Castel, would you mind if I sit with you?"

He did not rise, but nodded. "Sit, and welcome." She took the chair facing him and the wall behind him. Castel said, "What would you like to talk about? Or do you want silence?"

She shook her head. "Not silence—and any subject will do. No—first, I have a question. Who of you is most skilled in unarmed combat?"

He paused, and a girl served Rissa her breakfast. It was much as usual—meat, eggs, toasted buns, coffee, juice—except that here the dishes and cutlery were plain. She looked around and saw that others now eating were served equally well. A thought came; she said to Castel, "But should not this be yours? You have been waiting longer."

He laughed. "I've eaten. Don't worry—in this kitchen it's first come, first served. Of course the dining rooms have priority."

"I am glad that status does not intrude here. Now—my question?"

"Unarmed, you say? There's several good ones, but—remember Ernol? The dark one? I'd say he's the best, all around. But can I ask—why? I mean—excuse me if I misjudge you, but you must know you can't use a substitute in a duel."

Mouth full, unable to speak, she gestured. Then; "Of course not—what I need is someone to practice with. I have been shadowfighting, but that is only part of training and preparation."

"Ernol's your man, then. And don't worry—he'll take it easy; he won't hurt you."

Again, to swallow, she had to pause. "If he does not try his utmost, he will be no use to me. Will dal Nardo take it easy?"

"But—"

"Oh, we will—assuming Ernol is willing to help me—use practice rules. No deliberate disabling or mutilation, and so forth. But if he can throw me, I expect to land hard—if I do not, I shall be disappointed in him."

Castel grinned. "If Ernol throws you, not holding back, I guarantee you'll land hard enough to suit you!"

She had eaten rapidly; she mopped up the last of the egg, then filled her coffee cup again and rereplenished his half-full one. "That is good. Will you see Ernol, do you think, in the next hour or so?"

"I can, easy enough."

"Will you ask him if it is feasible—I do not know his duties —to practice with me this morning?" Castel nodded. "Then I will expect him—or word that he cannot meet me—at my door, in an hour or a little more."

"He'll be there. Oh—what type of combat suit should he bring?"

"Dal Nardo and I are to fight nude." She paused. "If Ernol does not wish to practice that way, he can wear briefs of the kind that are smooth and give no handhold—and I will, also, if he prefers." Another pause. "Oh, yes—ask him to bring wrestling-grease." Castel stared at her. "For my hair. No matter how I bound it, dal Nardo could dig in and find a grip. I cannot afford that."

"You could cut it."

"But I will not. And the grease has other advantages."

He shrugged. "It's your fight. All right—I'll have Ernol

report as soon as he can.''

"Thank you, Castel.'' She rose and would have picked up her dishes, but the young man took them himself, carrying them to a stacked counter. He waved a hand and left.

She paused to thank the cook, then went out. Sparline Moray sat alone in the dining room, drinking coffee; the remains of her breakfast had not yet been removed.

"Well, Rissa—where have you been? Liesel went into town first thing—said she'd eat when she got there—and Hawkman's still not come back. So, as you see, I had to eat alone.''

"I am sorry, but I was up early. No one was here. I was very hungry, so I ate in the kitchen.''

"I do that myself, sometimes. Learn anything interesting?''

"I have arranged, I think, for a partner to practice unarmed combat. I have been shadow-fighting, of course, but it is not the same as a real workout.''

"Whom have you picked?''

"The dark one called Ernol.''

Sparline thought, then nodded. "Oh, yes—he's very good. Sometimes we have contests—like tournaments—among our own people or with other houses. Ernol hasn't lost at his own weight or near it since—oh, maybe two years ago. You—are you sure he's the one you want? *I'd* be very cautious against him, even at my best—and I've had training he hasn't, yet.''

"The best is what I want. But—you know things Ernol does not? Would you, perhaps, work with me also, a time or two?''

Sparline shook her head. "I'm too rusty—out of shape— I haven't kept at it lately. A demonstration, maybe, if you like . . .''

"All right; we will see. I must go upstairs now and prepare.''

In her room she rummaged and found briefs and a halter; she put them in a carrying bag in case Ernol wished them worn. As an afterthought, she added a pair of thin plastic gloves. Then she lay on the bed, relaxing and waiting. The knock caught her dozing.

She came awake at once, rose and opened the door. "You

are prompt, Ernol. Shall we go?" He nodded; she picked up the bag and they walked downstairs and out of the Lodge.

The few times he had escorted her on walks, Ernol had been pleasant but not talkative. Now he said nothing. She looked up to his face—he was taller by nearly a head—and said, "I hope you do not mind working with me. I need to practice with someone, and both Sparline and Castel say you are the best here."

"I don't mind; I like to practice. I like to fight, too—but of course *now*—"

"Ernol—if Castel did not tell you, I want your full efforts, no holding back—as though practicing against your most skilled rival. You would not use maiming tactics, of course—and we will not, here. But otherwise—well, if you do not do your best, you will be of little help to me."

He looked at her. "I hope you know what you're asking. Well, we'll see."

"Yes. We will. Oh—is nude combat acceptable?"

"Well—I'm not used to it, with a woman. How to guard the crotch when the risk's all one way—the idea sets me off balance a little. But as long as it's just practice . . ."

"Are you sure? You will not be *entirely* safe there; that would not be realistic. You must be on guard."

"Same as with a man, yes. All right." He took her arm. "Over here's where we practice without clothes. Leave the gate shut, and nobody comes in."

With the gate closed behind them, they followed a path that wound through undergrowth and reached a clearing—round, level, its soil hard-packed. Ernol stripped without comment; Rissa did also. When she was done, she looked at him.

Clothed, he had looked slim, not especially powerful. Now she saw the width of shoulders compared to waist, the sleek muscles and flat belly. She nodded. "Certainly, Ernol, you have the physique to be great in combat."

"So do you. And if—if it weren't for status, I'd say more."

"I assume you mean a compliment; if so, I accept it. But we are here for practice."

"I know." His breathing was rapid. "I wish we weren't, though."

"You would be disappointed. I am not a responsive woman."

"Oh. Anyway, I guess I should apologize." His shoulders slumped.

"For what? You said nothing wrong. Now let us get on with it. First, will you rub the grease you brought into my hair so you can get no grip on it? Here—these gloves will keep your hands dry."

The grease felt clammy on her scalp, and on her back when he let her hair drop against it. "Make certain there are no twists or knots that fingers can catch in. That is the point of this tactic." He reassured her and stripped off the gloves; they stood and faced each other, about three paces apart. "Thank you, Ernol. We may begin—*now!*" But she did not move.

Nor did he; both waited. Well, if he would not start it, she would. She moved in short, slow steps—toward him, to one side, then the other, now back a step and—

Without warning his foot shot out; as she dropped to one side and rolled, the heel grazed her ear. She thought, *good! —he is really going to push me as hard as he can*. She barely escaped his following lunge—he *was* fast—and as he went past her, caught him under the ribs with a hand chop. He wheeled; again they faced, and he was smiling. "You *do* know what you're doing! I'm glad."

Then he rushed her, veiling intent with feints before his hand scythed at her neck. Her hunched shoulder caught the blow; she dodged away. Her heel caught his kneecap a token gouge as she flat-cartwheeled to come facing him, on hands and feet a moment before she sprang upright and circled to his left. "They told me truth, Ernol. You are very good indeed!"

Through the next passage, and another and another, they learned each other's ways. Panting more than he, from her disadvantage in size and reach, Rissa considered what she knew.

She ducked under his lunge, braced hands on the ground to one side, and plunged a foot at his moving body. He over-balanced and fell heavily, up again before she could follow her advantage—but she had made the first throw. Now, perhaps the spice of anger . . .

But he smiled again. "That move—I hadn't known it. You'll teach me later?" She nodded, and at that moment the pattern became clear to her.

Now she concentrated on learning what Ernol used, of the tactics she knew, and what he did not. She was sweating freely, breathing hard—her blood pumped hot and strong as she moved and countermoved, took blows and gave them. Pain came and went; she threw it off until later. But one thing was clear . . .

As she wove and dodged, struck and retreated, she knew her advantage over Ernol—he was very good at what he knew, but as she had predicted to Hawkman, she knew things he could not know.

Nor—she exulted—could dal Nardo!

Now she tried moves she knew to be recent developments on Earth at the time she had left it. Neither knowing nor expecting them, Ernol was vulnerable and could not counter, so she used only token force. After a time, both of them slowed by fatigue, he spread both hands wide and said, "I'm thirsty. And I caught your hair by mistake and can't hold on with this hand. Take a break?"

She panted; the last exchanges had been strenuous. "Yes, of course." At the edge of the clearing, while Ernol wiped his hand, she looked at her watch. "Ernol! I would not have believed it. Do you know we have been working for nearly an hour?"

She drank from their canteen, then waited while he took a few swallows. He said, "It didn't seem that long, but sure feels like it. You know something?"

"Possibly—but what you wish to tell me, I do not know."

"I didn't think you could stay with me this long. Nobody has, lately, my size or even a little bigger. You sure know stuff that I don't." He shook his head. "Maybe I'm not as good as I thought."

She touched his shoulder. "In the techniques you know, Ernol, you are superb. It is only that I come recently from Earth and have learned others." She laughed. "In fact, you used one new to me—and nearly took my head off!"

She saw him relax. "Then I don't have to feel ashamed,

to be stopped all the time by a little runt like you." His eyes widened. "Oh, hey—I'm sorry, Ms. Obrigo—I didn't mean—"

She laughed. "There is no offense—it is a fact that compared to you I am short in height. But I have had training that is not available to you on this planet."

"You said—you'll teach me?"

"Gladly." She moved her shoulders and winced. "I do not know about you, Ernol, but I think I have had enough for today. My muscles complain."

She saw him looking at the bruise on her rib cage and the lower part of her left breast. "Hey," he said, "I didn't mean to get you on the tit that way. But you jumped, you see, and I—"

She shook her head. "No apologies, Ernol. We stayed with practice rules and still had a good hard session of it, so we bear the marks. But neither of us is truly injured. It was a good workout, and I thank you. Has your nose finished bleeding from when I had to butt in order to break free?"

"Just about."

"Good." She started to gather her clothing. "We had better get back to the Lodge and wash ourselves."

"There's a stream a little further along. It's chilly, but that's good after a workout like this."

She had pictured soaking in a hot tub, but . . . "All right."

He led the way; soon the path reached a mossy stream bank. "It is wide enough for swimming," she said. "How deep?"

"To my waist. The current's fairly strong—but steady, not tricky. And a sandy bottom here—good footing." Suddenly he shouted, "Last one in's a frunk!"

She had no chance—with the first word he leaped, a flat dive, and then a sharp turn to avoid the opposite bank. He stood and splashed up at her; laughing, she took a step and jumped, feet first, pulling up her knees to land spraddled and make a huge splash. She went under, rolled and put her feet down to come up standing, braced against the current and facing him. She shook her head to free her eyes of water. "Chilly, did you say? I think you would have to warm it to freeze it!" She lay forward and swam a few strokes upstream, working hard but barely making headway.

She stood again, panting now, waded to the bank and squatted beside Ernol in the shallower water. As he was doing, she began rubbing herself with the fine bottom-sand—first arms and legs, then her body. Several places, when she touched them, caused her to wince. Before she was finished, the chill had her teeth chattering.

"Oh, damn all! Ernol—like a fool I forgot to bring anything to take the grease off my head."

"On this kind, sand works fine."

"Perhaps—but the time it would take, I would be frozen stiff."

"Yes, you're right. Here, let me squeeze out the worst, what I can. Then you can get out." From the forehead he pushed his palms over her scalp, pressing hard until he reached the nape. He repeated the action, then grasped her hair at that point and pulled his hand, squeezing, down the rest of it. He showed her the blobs of grease on his hands. "See? You'll still have to clean up, but that's most of it." She scrambled onto the bank, shivering; he used more sand on his hands, then joined her. "Come on—let's run back—warm up a little."

He set out, sprinting. She followed, but he was faster; she fell behind. When she reached the arena she was breathing hard and felt almost warm again, but the clearing's sunlight was welcome.

Hands on hips, Ernol stood grinning. "You like my bath place?"

"It is . . . invigorating. While one lasts." She began to dress; after a moment, he did also. She said, "Do you suppose it is time for lunch? I am hungry."

"If it isn't, join us in the kitchen. Snacks available at any time."

"Perhaps I will—though I need to talk with the Hulzeins, and seldom except at mealtimes do I find them free."

"Well—any time, remember. Ready to go?"

"Yes." On the way to the Lodge, Ernol lapsed again into silence, and Rissa found no reason to break it. They entered the building at the rear; where their ways parted and they said brief good-byes. "And thank you again, Ernol." He only nodded.

Going to her room, she encountered no one. She decided hunger could wait; she stripped and had her delayed hot tub, scrubbing the rest of the grease from her hair and then lying relaxed, letting the heat loosen muscles and soothe bruises. All in all, she thought, the morning had been quite productive.

THE bath's controls kept the water hot; after a time she fell into reverie. When the knock came she had no idea how long she had lain there. On the intercom she asked, "Who is it?"

"Sparline."

"Oh—come in, please. I am in the bath."

"Hungry? I am."

"Yes. I will dress immediately and join you."

"No, stay put—I'll have something sent up for us." Rissa heard her talking to someone, but could not make out the words. Then Sparline entered and sat in a chair near the tub. "Well—did you have a good session?" She looked more closely. "Ouch! I'll say you did! I guess you didn't do so well?"

"I am most satisfied—these marks you see are not serious, and Ernol carries about as many. He strikes beautifully and is quick of mind as well as body—with equal training he would beat me every time, or nearly. But as it is I outthrew him almost two to one, and never could he immobilize me. Nor vice versa, for that matter—his strength and skills together are too great. I relied on quickness—we are roughly equal—and my added training."

"Are you ready for dal Nardo?"

"I would like another session or two, possibly one with a larger partner, then a day of relaxation. Then—I will be ready, yes."

Sparline frowned. "Maybe we can get him to grant a postponement."

Rissa sat upright; a small tidal wave splashed down the length of the bath to rebound against her. "The time is set? But, Hawkman—"

"He's not back yet. And dal Nardo's seconds were insistent, so Liesel acted for you. She agreed to the day after tomorrow. And if Hawkman isn't here to second you, I'll do it. I and another."

"Who is the other?"

Sparline shook her head. "I don't know—it's Liesel who said it."

Rissa started to lean back again, then changed her mind and sprang out, dripping. Taking a large towel, she walked into the bedroom section. Sparline followed. "Rissa—I'm sorry. If you're not prepared, we can—"

"No." As she dried herself, the warmed towel soothed her skin. "It will be in two days, as agreed. I am ready enough— and if not, it is my own fault. It is only that—as a principal, I suppose I expected to be consulted, on terms." A knock came. "Well, enough—that will be one with food. I will answer."

She wrapped the towel around her. At the door she accepted a tray from the girl who brought it, thanked her, and took the food to a small table by the window. "Let us sit down, shall we?"

Exercise improved Rissa's appetite; she ate half again as much as usual, finishing all that Sparline left in the serving dishes. Then she touched a napkin to her mouth, leaned back, and said, "Now—what circumstances are agreed? The place, and the rest of it?"

"An arena by the spaceport—neutral ground, neither ours nor dal Nardo's. It's fenced against the curious, but not roofed. The surface is bare soil, well packed. The terms, though—"

"Yes?"

"There'll be more people than I'd like. Dal Nardo insisted on five of his own, including his seconds, so we'll have the same. Then the referee and two assistants—all armed, but no one else will be. Plus the doctor and one aide. That makes— let's see—seventeen, all told. I could do with less—the last time Hawkman fought, there weren't more than—oh, about a dozen, I'd guess.''

Rissa shrugged. "Excess spectators are not important."

Leaning forward, Sparline frowned. "Claques are dangerous. They shout advice, they distract—they can misdirect their principal's opponent.''

"Yes, I see." Rissa nodded. "In combat one could take wrong advice by mistaking one voice for another. Very well—now that I am warned, I shall plan to pay no heed to *any*.''

She smiled. "Sparline, this will be to *our* advantage. Let our group shout advice, true and false, both to me and aimed at dal Nardo. He will think I listen and respond to what I hear; therefore he will have to pay heed to all of it. I will not—I can put full attention to him, to him alone!"

Sparline's eyes widened. "You—in seconds, you turn dal Nardo's strategy against him! I begin to think—''

"That I will live? But how can you doubt it? I—I—" Suddenly her mouth warped into a grimace; tears flowed. She put her hands to her face, shaking her head violently. Sparline came and embraced her; against the warm bosom the jerking head quieted, but Rissa's sobbing took longer to abate. Then she pushed away, gently, wiped her eyes and met Sparline's gaze.

"There is no point in fooling others, is there? I pretend well, I think, that I am confident—but I do not fool myself. In truth, I am terrified, when I allow myself to feel it. Not of pain, but that deliberately, out of his vengeful whim, that man may stop my life. And before I have done—oh, so many things I may never have the chance to do. I wish—well, never mind. Either I shall do them or, being dead, I shall not."

Sparline clutched Rissa's shoulder. "You need a drink." She reached for the brandy flask; a moment later Rissa was sipping from its cap. Her lips still trembled.

"Want to talk about it a little more?"

"No." Then Rissa paused, and said, "Today. I find myself wishing I had opened to Ernol's friendly lust. But I did not."

"You mean he—?"

"He was not offensive—do not think that. He was—complimentary, and obviously available. There is no cause for displeasure.''

Smiling, Sparline stroked Rissa's hair. ''No—he's in no trouble—not for that. Rissa—once when I practiced nude combat with a man alone—well, it didn't stop there. The excitement and all—you know?'' She laughed. ''What I'm saying is, there's lots of precedent. And—you know—there's nothing like it, really.''

Rissa wanted to smile but could not. ''Walking back here together, he did not speak.''

Sparline stood. ''You want me to send him up to you?''

''No. It would not be the same, would it?''

''I guess not. Anything else I can help with?'' Rissa shook her head; Sparline smiled and left. The door, closing, sounded to Rissa like the end of something.

She moved to pour herself another cap of brandy, drank half of it, and then sat on the bed, taking the rest a tongue-taste at a time. After a while the thought came that it had been more than half her lifetime since last she had cried.

After all, a few stray, silent tears did not count—did they?

ALL afternoon Rissa did not leave her room. For nearly an hour she exercised, loosening and stretching her muscles. She read parts of her notes and made a few additions. She watched through the window as sunlight shifted and changed the look of what she saw. She poured more brandy but set it aside; when she next remembered it and sipped, the strong spirit was no longer to her taste. No matter—it would keep.

She thought of things she had done and not done, and wondered which she might regret if she allowed herself that feeling. In that light she reviewed her first meeting with dal Nardo—and then again. Finally, she said aloud, ''No. If it could be done again for the first time, all would be the same.''

With that conclusion came peace. She sat to write a coded letter to Erika. To Frieda, really, she knew—but as she wrote, it was Erika's face, Erika's reactions that she visualized. She sealed the letter and sat quietly, watching twilight approach.

YOUNG RISSA

• • •

LIESEL and Sparline shared dinner with her. After she gave Sparline her letter, for enclosure with the next batch of Earth-bound messages, she spoke little and listened only vaguely to what was said. Finally, after the meal, Liesel jogged her elbow. "Rissa? Are you asleep sitting up?"

Shaking her head, "No—preoccupied, I suppose. I am sorry."

"Well. I asked, just now, your plans for tomorrow."

"Exercise, of course, and rest. And—I had almost forgotten—collect my fee from Alsen Bleeker."

"Yes—and you'll need an escort. You can fly an aircar?"

"I have not for some time, and these are somewhat different from Erika's, but I believe I can manage. Why?"

"Then you won't need a pilot; that's all. And what with Sparline and I being busy, we'd be hard put to find you one."

"Who goes with me, then?"

"Do you have any preference, yourself?"

"Perhaps Ernol, who practice-fought so well with me to-day?"

"Hmm—you want an armed person. Ernol's adequate with weapons, but not the expert that some others are."

"It will not matter. A man of Hulzein Lodge, visibly armed—there should be no trouble."

Liesel nodded. "All right, I'll have him notified. He can spot Bleeker's building for you—it's on the edge of town so you won't need to know the traffic patterns, this trip. Now—what time?"

"To leave here? An hour before mid-morning should do."

"Then that's settled. Now the next thing—at the duel you're entitled to have your two seconds and three more of our people. Preferences?" Rissa shook her head. "Well, then—your seconds are Hawkman if he can get there, or Sparline if he can't, and one person of Hawkman's choice—he hasn't said who. I'd like to join you, but I can't. Two reasons—it's against custom for the prime head of this Lodge to appear for a connection not of blood or marriage. Also—one of us has to be here at our control center, and especially now. So—who else?"

She thought. "Sparline, if that is proper, even if Hawkman comes as my second. Ernol again, I think. You choose the rest."

Sparline turned to her mother. "The big man—what's his name?—who stunned a charging bushstomper with his fist. He's not fast, but if it came up necessary to intervene, he's big enough to hold dal Nardo."

"That's Splieg," said Liesel. "Good choice. And—how about Lebeter, the little knife artist?"

"But I thought," said Rissa, "that we must all be unarmed."

Sparline laughed. "Liesel, you think of everything! Rissa— he *will* be unarmed, but dal Nardo won't quite believe so."

"Come to think of it," said Liesel, "neither would I." She laughed. "Rissa, Sparline told me of your plan to turn dal Nardo's claque scheme against him. I like it—and if there's a place for Lebeter, he's another arrow to that same bow."

Rissa nodded. "I see the advantage of a teamwork of minds. Now when the time comes, I shall not feel so alone."

Liesel reached to grasp her shoulder. "Except for the fight itself—nobody can do *that* for you—you won't be. And if you fail, I promise—Hulzein Lodge promises—dal Nardo won't outlive you much."

Rissa looked at her. "Since I would not be here to see it, that prospect should not concern me. But—but it *does*—not that he would die, but that you would care enough to see that he did." She shook her head, blinking; no one would see tears from her again that day. "I will do without a liqueur tonight and go to my room. To meditate, perhaps, and clear my mind. Thank you both, and good night."

But in her room she saw the brandy she had poured earlier, and sat holding it, looking out at the night. When the flask cap was empty, she filled it again. The peace of meditation escaped her; her thoughts roiled and would not be quiet.

Finally, preparing for bed, she resorted to the stopgap

method of pushing her several turmoils into mental compartments and closing them firmly. Then she lay down and soon slept.

SHE woke unconvinced either of her own reality or her situation's. Mechanically she prepared for the day. After breakfast —served in her room, for she wished to talk with none—she sat and waited quietly until her departure time. Then she went downstairs and outside, to the aircar. Ernol, waiting beside it, greeted her. She saw the handgun at his belt.

"Good morning, Ernol. I hope you do not mind going to the city?"

"No. Makes a nice change. But why me? Lots of people here can outpoint me with guns." They climbed into the aircar; she inspected the controls.

"I doubt the gun will be needed—what kind is it, anyway? And I prefer your company to that of a stranger."

"Well, thanks. I'd . . . wondered." He touched the weapon. "This here? Nothing fancy—projectile type, like they've been making a long time, but this model throws more and faster than most. Expanding slug—really messy when it hits."

"Then I also *hope* it will not be needed. But our mission is supposedly peaceful." She started the propelling motors and let them idle. "And in a few moments, we are ready."

"Yes. You're sure you know how to run this thing?"

"If I were not, I would not try. Are you anxious?"

"No—just wondering, was all. I'm ready if you are."

"All right." She applied power; the car rose smoothly, and soon she had crossed the gap and turned parallel to the great hills, toward the city. For a time they rode without speaking; then she said, "Ernol? Yesterday—back in my room—I was sorry I had not accepted what you offered of yourself."

She waited. He cleared his throat and said, "Well, I knew I shouldn't be pushing against status. So it didn't bother me then—*before*. But after we'd fought such a good one, and then in the stream and on the way back . . . still, you say you don't respond, so—"

"Response or not, I am skilled. I would have pleased you." The aircar came out from under cloud; she squinted against sudden brightness. "My regret is that I might die tomorrow without pleasing someone who, by fighting me so well, pleased *me* a great deal."

"You mean you want to—"

"Not now—you said it correctly. After we practiced, when we were close from sharing that fight—then was the time. Perhaps someday, if I live and circumstances allow . . ."

"You want to practice this afternoon?"

"I cannot. As I said, the duel is set for tomorrow—and if you will, I would like you to be one of my party."

"Sure. It's—I'm honored."

"Thank you. But you see I cannot risk, so close to the event, even minor injury that might slow me against dal Nardo."

"Yesterday would have been just as bad, and you fought then."

"I did not know that terms were set, that it would be so soon."

He whistled. "Hey! Lucky we *didn't* get you a bad one. Because for sure I wasn't easing it any. You either, that I noticed."

She laughed. "No—we took all normal risks of practice. As you say, I was lucky." Approaching at an angle past the spaceport, they neared One Point One. "Ernol—from here, can you point out Alsen Bleeker's headquarters?"

"Yes—see the big building there, with the flags and towers? His is right behind it—you can land in the space between. See it?"

She swung left and nodded, and began her descent. Landing midway between the buildings she taxied to within a few yards of Bleeker's; they left the aircar and walked toward it.

"Where do we go in, Ernol?" Two small entrances faced them.

"Door on the left will get us there. Main entrance, if you'd rather, is on the other side."

"This will do." Once inside, stairs led them to a lobby, then an elevator to the fifth floor.

"The number's five-twenty-two," said Ernol, "but the whole floor's one big office, with cubbyholes along one side for the clerks."

"You have been here before, then."

"Once, with Hawkman Moray. But not armed—just for sideshow."

The elevator door opened. "This may not be a sideshow," said Rissa, "but I hope it is nothing more." She walked ahead to the door labeled "522" and opened it. "Let us find out."

The room was big; several yards away, behind a desk, sat a young male receptionist. Beyond him, through a transparent partition, Rissa saw Alsen Bleeker at his own desk. She walked directly toward Bleeker's door. The young man stood and raised a warding hand. "Just a moment—who are you?"

Passing his desk, Rissa ignored him. Peripherally she saw Ernol touch his handgun; the young man sat again. Over her shoulder, she said, "We are expected."

Bleeker did not look as though he expected anyone; startled, he raised his head and jerked it toward Ernol. "Who told you, Ms. Obrigo, to bring a gunman?"

"I told you I would be escorted. Under the circumstances, Hulzein Lodge would hardly allow me into this city without protection."

"Well, it doesn't matter—I have protection of my own." Bleeker's eyes flicked to one side; Rissa turned to see a man standing in an alcove. She suppressed a gasp.

Low-voiced, she said to Ernol, "That's Blaise Tendal."

"I know him. If this is ambush, I hope you're armed—he's faster than me."

She touched his arm. "Never mind—likely it will not come to that." To Bleeker she said, "I see that you consort with my enemies."

In his lip-stretching way, Bleeker smiled. "I hire the best talent."

"That is yet to be seen," said Rissa. "But—we have business."

"In a minute, maybe," said Tendal. He walked across the

room. On solid footing, Rissa thought, the man was almost obscenely graceful; he suggested fluid rippling in a shallow pool.

Tendal stood with one hip propped on Bleeker's desk. "We have some business, too," he said. "And you, there, with your one little gun—don't interfere."

"I see three weapons on you," said Ernol. "Maybe more, hidden. Why do you need so much? You have just two hands, the same as me."

Bleeker tried to speak but Rissa overrode him. "*My* escort will do his job—nothing more. Does yours take orders or does he not?"

Tendal laughed. "You'll find out. I—"

Memory came to her. "Swallow your tongue, Tendal! We are not here to listen to you—do your job or give place to someone who will!"

The man came upright. His hand moved toward a weapon, but Bleeker reached and grasped his arm. "Damn you, Blaise! Are you trying to ruin me? Kill her here, and we're *all* dead."

Tendal shrugged the hand away. "All right—I'll play your games—for now." He pushed himself up and sat fully on the desk, arms hanging free at his sides. Bleeker glowered, but Tendal did not see.

Rissa spoke. "If your tedious employee is done parading himself, Bleeker, there is a matter of payment. Can we get to it?"

"Yes, of course." Bleeker held out a paper. "Here is your certificate."

She inspected it. "Your own private money? I expected Weltmarks, negotiable anywhere."

"A Hulzein connection and you don't know about house certificates? Read it—convertible on demand, after five days; or at *any* time—with a six-to-five advantage—into shares of the Bleeker holdings. I assure you, Ms. Obrigo, this certificate is legal tender anywhere on Number One."

She looked to Ernol; he nodded. "He's right, there. It's not a snick."

"All right, then." She turned again to Bleeker. "Is this also how you will pay off our wager?"

She saw his smile again and wished she had not. He said, "Let's say that's the form my stakes are in. I don't expect to be paying—or to see you again."

"No?" Turning, she prepared to leave. "A number of things happen, I would imagine, that you do not expect. Good-bye, Bleeker." She began to walk away, Ernol beside her.

"Hold on, there!" Both wheeled—Blaise Tendal stood, tight-grinned, his clawed hands a few inches from his sides. "All right, One-Gun—*you're* not status-protected—let's see who's best. I'll use just one gun, too—but guess which!"

Rissa did not pause. As Tendal's gun came up, adrenaline shock struck her and time slowed. She made a dive—not directly toward him, but at an angle. She landed on both palms, skidded only slightly and pivoted, throwing her body and legs around at Tendal. Her shins caught his ankles like a scythe.

The gun fired; slugs ricocheted around the room; he fell across and past her. She twisted and came up to see Ernol with both hands at Tendal's throat. Bleeker came forward, around the desk; Rissa waved him back and gripped Ernol's neck from behind, shaking it.

"*Ernol!* Hold him, yes—but do not strangle him completely—while I take his weapons, all of them." Ernol nodded; she released her grip. Searching Tendal she found three guns, two knives, and an object she could not classify but kept anyway. She held one gun and put the rest in the shoulder bag she had dropped when she attacked. Then she paused and saw that Blaise Tendal was only half-conscious. "You can let go now, Ernol. I have a gun to control him."

Ernol let the man slump to the floor, then stood and flexed his hands. "I told you—I'm not much with guns. Didn't even try to use mine, just my hands. I'm sorry."

"Do not be. I knew when I chose you that you are not primarily oriented to weapons. But I thought it would be all right." She shrugged. "And it *is* all right." She turned to Bleeker. "This breach of procedure will interest Hulzein Lodge. And I shall not speak in your favor." She turned again to leave.

Bleeker, his voice high and strained, said, "Wait! Ms. Obrigo, I didn't—this wasn't supposed to happen. I—"

"Was it not? I wonder. But—very well—I will not speak against you, either. I—and Ernol—will merely report what occured.

"Now, if there is nothing more, we must take our leave." This time Bleeker said nothing.

A thought made her hesitate. She looked at Tendal, sitting up and holding his throat, his eyes vacant. "You! You did not know or intend it, but you have done me a favor. But not one on which you can presume." She looked more closely and decided he could understand her words. Making a decision, she nodded. "Listen to me, Blaise Tendal. This is the second time you have threatened me and lived. It is also the last."

Now she turned away for the last time; the two left the big room and then the building. Outside as they walked to the air-car, passing clouds interrupted sunshine.

ALOFT, once again in sunlight, she thought of what had happened. Yes—it was for the best; it was what she had needed. Until Ernol spoke, she had forgotten his presence.

"You said—Tendal did you a *favor?* I don't see how."

"It was a kind of practice you could not give me."

"But how—?"

She laughed. "There is a response I have to real danger, that I had not had in so long that I did not know whether I could count on it, against dal Nardo. The adrenaline that comes in life danger—it affects me so that time seems to slow and nothing but the immediate peril exists. I do not really move that much faster, I think—but it seems as if there is many times as long, to decide and act, than is truly the case.

"In the practice—it was good fighting but I *knew* you would not kill me. But when Tendal's gun came out—to me it was minutes, rather than seconds, before my legs cut him down. I do not suppose this makes any sense to you, Ernol —to most people it does not."

Abruptly, he laughed. "Not make sense? Sure it does." He laughed again, more quietly. "How do you think I got to his throat so fast?"

She checked the centering of her controls for level flight, then turned to look at him. "The extra adrenaline does not go away immediately, does it?"

"It sure doesn't. I—"

"Ernol. This, now—it is much like yesterday, after we fought. Is it not?" She did not wait for answer; looking ahead and down she said, "I see a clearing where we might land. Do you mind if our lunch at the Lodge is somewhat delayed?"

AIRBORNE again, now approaching the Lodge, Ernol said, "I see what you meant. You made it great for me—better than anybody—but I couldn't for you, could I?"

"It is my own lack, Ernol—no one has done better. And I enjoyed very much the pleasure I could give you." She sighed. "Let us drop the matter—except to keep good memories of each other."

"Not again, then?"

"I would not think so. Unless, if ever we practice-fight again ...."

"Yes, maybe. But it doesn't matter—I'll fight for you anytime—against anybody."

"Of course. And I for you—as we did today." They smiled together.

WHEN she landed, Ernol said, "I'll see you tomorrow, then," and started toward the rear entrance.

"No—come with me. We have a report to make." He turned and followed her inside. It was past lunch time, but they found Liesel and Sparline still in the dining room, lingering over coffee.

Liesel looked up. "Took you long enough. Anything special happen?"

"A few things. We are hungry. May Ernol, who has fought for me today, eat with me also, while we tell you?"

Liesel grinned. "Sure—our protocol's not *that* strict." She rang for service.

A boy entered and Rissa chose her meal. Ernol said nothing; she looked to him. "Would you like the same?" He nodded. "Two orders, then, but add extra helpings to his, please."

Rissa began her account, occasionally checking details with Ernol. The food came, and for once she talked while eating. Meal and story ended at about the same time; the serving-boy removed the dishes and poured more coffee. When he had gone, Liesel asked, "You think Bleeker wanted Tendal to kill you, and protested only so Ernol could witness for him?"

"I do not know. Perhaps Bleeker himself does not. He is not, I think, very intelligent. Cunning, yes—but short-sighted."

"How do you mean?" Sparline said.

"The tool he chose—Blaise Tendal. Hawkman was right; the man is not sane—nor reliable. He tried for Ernol first—and with his witness dead, how would Bleeker stand?"

Liesel nodded. "And more than that—probably Tendal would've made a clean sweep, *including* Bleeker. His record isn't one of moderation."

For the first time, except to answer, Ernol spoke. "How many kills does he have?"

Sparline said, "I'm not sure. More than twenty, though."

Ernol's fist tapped the table. "That's too many."

"You think to challenge him?" Sparline shook her head. "You've never killed, have you, Ernol? No—I know you haven't. But you can't do it, anyway—his dal Nardo marriage puts him out of status range."

"That's a mock marriage! Everybody knows it!"

"Yes," said Liesel. "But binding, all the same."

"If the dal Nardos can do it—" He looked to Sparline. "You're not married. No disrespect—I wouldn't presume—afterward you'd annul it and I'd leave so things wouldn't be awkward. But—"

Sparline patted his hand. "Ernol, you're a dear young man—I'm fond of you, and I expect you'd be a lovely romp. And I'm *most* pleased with what you did today. But no marriage of mine will be a mock one. And besides, I'm *too* fond of you to help you go up against a twenty-plus killer."

He pulled his hand away. "If I've offended—"

Liesel made a brief snort of laughter. "Offended? Peace, no! Initiative never offends me—unless it's irresponsible, and yours isn't. You want to know the truth, I'm *touched*—and that's rare."

She scowled at nothing. "Tomorrow morning, Ernol—no, the next day, after this mess is settled—come to my office. All right?"

"Yes, of course. But—"

"You're wondering why? You can handle more responsibility than you've had. We'll discuss your new promotion, is all."

He looked down at his hands. "Thank you. Maybe I should go now. Work to do."

"You've *done* a good day's work," said Liesel, "but all right."

He rose and walked toward the kitchen. Rissa called after him, "My thanks again, Ernol. I will see you tomorrow morning—and well rested, I hope." He nodded but did not turn.

LIESEL shook her head. "All this young talent, and I never have time to keep tabs on who deserves a better job. Rissa, I'm glad you spotted this one for me before he got totally stuck in the servant mentality."

"He's not stuck in anything," said Sparline. "He follows status rules, is all. Raise his status, and he'll adjust like a shot."

"Rissa, what do you think?"

"Your status system, Liesel, is not clear to me. But about Ernol, Sparline is right. He has great potential."

"Well. Good." Liesel stood. "Back to work for me, too. Still no word from Hawkman; maybe I'll find his call on record." She walked away, into the hall and then out of sight.

F. M. Busby

Rissa's coffee was cold, and she wanted no more. She felt drained, unready for the exercising she had planned. She sat, aware of Sparline's gaze but saying nothing.

Finally the other spoke. "The times don't fit."

"Pardon?"

"You met Bleeker, this and that happened—not to slight what *did* happen—you came out, and that's all. Took you a long time to get home, I think. How'd you go—via the Slab Jumbles?"

"No." Sparline's concerned expression belied her flippant words. "We stopped on the way—there was a clearing. I rectified my omission of yesterday. And I am glad I did."

"So I guessed right about him!"

"A lovely romp, you said? Very much so—or he would be, if—you see, my body has never responded fully to any man."

"Rissa, I—I mean—"

"Nor to any woman, for that matter. But my gladness— that is for Ernol's pleasure in our coupling."

Sparline's laugh was shaky. "I didn't know—I'm sorry. But as long as you didn't feel you were being *used*—"

"I have been used before; perhaps I will be again. But it is *not* mere use when it is of my own choice."

"No—I suppose not. Well—as Ernol said, and Liesel— there's work to do. Excuse me?" Rissa looked after her, wondering if she had said too much. Finally she shrugged —did it matter?

IN her room she dressed for exercise. Outdoors, she deliberately ran herself out of breath—then, panting, she practiced the most demanding of her skills. She leaped and dove, fell and landed rolling; she swung her legs in kicks that stretched tendons near to pain. Against a thick tree trunk she made the high kick that somersaulted her backward to land crouched, facing the tree to kick again or change attack if need be. Never did she pause to catch breath, but soon her lungs caught up to her pace and she knew she would not lose to fatigue.

YOUNG RISSA

She ran again—not sprinting now but moving easily—bobbing and turning, stretching herself free of tensions, breathing long and deeply to fill her lungs with the moist, clear air. When she had enough and turned for a final run back to the Lodge, she could not feel a stiff or sore muscle. Aside from a few bruises, she realized, she had not felt so fit since her training days at Erika's.

Back in her room, she bathed—but in water not much more than tepid, rather than the heat of the day before. She was on a fine edge now; too deep a relaxation might lose it. There was a balance, she had learned—now was the time to keep it, very carefully.

Emotionally that balance was precarious; she decided not to risk it. She sent word to Liesel that she would take dinner and next morning's breakfast alone in her room. And she placed her orders for those meals—what she would have, and when.

The rest of the evening, except for eating dinner, she spent in meditation. And now, rather than shutting her anxieties away, she was able to dissolve them. An early hour found her ready for sleep.

RISSA woke slowly, stretched and yawned. She rolled over to doze longer; then the thought stabbed her: *It's today!* She spread her limbs, muscles flaccid, until the premature adrenaline subsided. Then she rose and began to prepare.

Her nails were shorter than she wished; she filed those of thumbs and middle fingers to the best points she could manage, and cut the rest short.

Her breakfast, a light meal but sustaining, came on schedule. She had a free hour before departure time; she used it leisurely, and when she went downstairs, found herself untroubled by the thought that she might never see that room again.

She listened, heard voices from the dining room and smiled. Of course—where else would they be?

Five awaited her; she felt disappointment that none was

Hawkman. Liesel, Sparline, Ernol, and two strangers. The large one, built like a bear—that would be Splieg, who pole-axed bushstompers with his bare fist. The smaller, thin-faced with a crooked nose, must be Lebeter the knifester.

Before any could greet her, she raised a hand. "Good morning, and let me say something quickly. For what is to come, the mental state—the concentration—is most important. So with no thought of discourtesy, may I ask that none speak to me until we are in the arena, and then only of the combat itself?"

One by one they nodded. Low-voiced, Liesel said to the others, "She's right. I've heard of this—never saw it before, though. All right, I'll say no more."

She led the way outside and to an aircar larger than the ones Rissa had seen here before. "You're familiar with this model, Lebeter?" The man nodded. Liesel put a hand to Rissa's shoulder, squeezed once, then turned and walked away.

Lebeter took the pilot's chair; Splieg sat beside him, leaving the broad rear seat for Rissa to sit between Ernol and Sparline.

The sun was bright, the clouds few as Lebeter took them through the gap and turned toward One Point One. Rissa felt the weight of the silence she had imposed; in her peripheral vision she saw Sparline and Ernol watching her. Unable to be comfortable, she wriggled. Finally she took Sparline's hand on one side and Ernol's on the other. After a few moments she noticed that all three were breathing deeply and in unison. For the rest of the ride she relaxed with closed eyes.

THE aircar landed; they approached the arena, a fenced enclosure with guarded gate. Sparline looked in first, turned and said, "Hawkman's inside. I'm afraid we brought you to no purpose, Lebeter—sorry. Roam as you will, but stay fairly near the aircar—we may be leaving in more hurry than we expect." The man waved a hand in half-salute and walked to sit beside the car, his back against a landing wheel.

"Formation," said Sparline. Rissa found herself surrounded as they walked forward and through the gate—Sparline and Ernol in front and Splieg behind.

Inside, as she strove to make a pattern, to identify those present, there was no help to relaxation. She first saw—and heard—dal Nardo; at the far side he shouted at a black-robed figure flanked by two in gray. Sparline muttered, "Harassing the referee already, is he?"

Alongside dal Nardo, Rissa saw two men and a woman, none familiar to her. And half-hidden, behind a hulking shape entirely cloaked in robe and hood, stood Blaise Tendal. She blinked and saw Hawkman Moray approaching, followed by a tallish, slim man wearing a mask-hood. Hawkman and Sparline clasped hands, and he said, "We'd better do it. You tell her." Rissa could not hear her reply.

She looked further. The other two—the woman in white was, of course, the doctor, and beside her Rissa saw a girl with short tousled fair hair. The girl turned and she recognized her briefly-met friend, Felcie Parager. Felcie's eyes went wide.

"Oh, Tari! I was afraid it might be you—but I hoped it wasn't!"

"Breach of terms!" Dal Nardo roared it. "Officials supposed to be neutral! I claim foul!"

Felcie cringed. "Sir—I didn't mean anything—I only—"

Some things, thought Rissa, are more important than keeping to a plan. She pitched her voice to carry. "Claim and be damned to you! The girl expressed nothing outside the rules." In the sudden quiet she said, using a more normal tone, "And shut your great mouth. Your bellowing is not seemly before the event proceeds." She turned away, disturbed to find herself near to shaking with rage. She could not afford this much stimulation so early—she took deep, slow breaths and began to calm again.

Sparline took her arm and leaned to speak softly. "Not to distract you, but afterward—after you *win*, Rissa!—don't be alarmed, or hesitate, at what you're asked to do. It's politically important, and no demand on you. All right?"

Confused, Rissa said, "I suppose so—I trust you." An arm hugged her shoulders and she looked up to see Hawkman's smile.

"All right, are you?" he said. "I've heard good things of you." He moved away and consulted with the black-robed referee. Then that person spoke.

"It is time. Tari Obrigo challenges Stagon dal Nardo, to the death. Weapons, none. Clothing, none. Seconds and other agreed parties are present. Now, if they wish, the opponents may speak. Challenged party speaks first."

Wearing a maroon robe, dal Nardo stalked to the edge of the marked circle. Beside him, covered by a shapeless cloak and hood, came the person none had seen. "Here's what I can do," said dal Nardo. "You'll see! But first I'll tell you, Tari Obrigo—you walking piece of fertilizer!" He laughed, and to Rissa the sound came like the stench of death.

Then he talked. One by one he named the parts of her and what he would do to them—break this, crush that, bite away one thing, gouge out another—on and on, his harsh voice rising as he detailed a vivisection by hands and teeth. Then he paused and laughed again. "Maybe you don't believe. I'll show you. Here's what I do only in *practice*!" And he pulled the cloak off the creature beside him.

The sounds from those around her drowned Rissa's gasp. Dal Nardo's exhibit was a woman, tall and muscular—but she looked as though she might be better dead. Blood dribbled from a puffed, purpled socket that might or might not still hold an eye. Bare, bloody patches marked the scalp. Bruises and gaping cuts covered limbs and torso; one breast hung—a flattened, blackened mass—half-torn from the chest. An arm swung crookedly; the gaping mouth showed only a few broken teeth behind swollen, bloody lips. Below a raw cut closed by crude stitches, blood also stained the belly. And—and—shaking her head, Rissa closed her eyes and turned away. Dizzied, she fought to hold her vomit.

A supporting hand gripped her arm; Sparline's whisper hissed in her ear. "It's a *fake*, most of it! Plastic and make-up! I recognize her—a professional kill-fighter from the Twin Worlds—she had only one breast when she came here; that messy-looking thing is pure phony. And the belly—the stitches are real, but the wound isn't. Same with the eye, I'll bet. The arm's real—I hope she charged him plenty to let him break it. Rissa—?''

Her eyes opened; she straightened and shook her head. ''Thank you—I am all right now. He is truly worth killing, is he not?''

Again dal Nardo spoke—now of what he would do while his opponent was helpless but not yet dead. ''Top and bottom, fore and aft—''

She turned to Sparline. ''This, that he says, is legal?''

''If death is, so's rape. That's how the code sees it, anyway.''

''I—did not know. Is it, soon, my time to speak?''

Across the way, it was dal Nardo who answered. ''I'm finished. If the fertilizer wants to squeak like a mouse, I can wait and hear her out.''

Rissa stepped forward, so that none stood between them. She paused—was it worth her while to speak? *Yes!* She nodded.

Then she spoke. ''As when I first met you, dal Nardo, you talk a great deal. I shall waste less time than you. If I squeak like a mouse, you—as I told you at our first meeting—shit like a bull, but from your mouth.'' She saw his face swell and redden. ''Ah—I anger you. That is good—your blood near the surface, easier to shed.''

She breathed deeply—it was nearly time, now, and she would need reserve oxygen. ''Thank you for warning me of your sexual intent. I shall make certain you are unable to fulfill it.''

She paused once more, then shook her head. ''That is all. Let us prepare and meet.'' She turned to Sparline. ''The grease—on my hair, a great deal of it.'' She stripped and stood, air moving against her skin, while Sparline rubbed the oily gel into her scalp and down her hanging hair.

''His belly looks tempting,'' said Sparline, ''but don't bother. Under that fat, he's rock hard.'' Rissa nodded.

Ernol said, ''Look! She's putting adhesive on his hands!'' Rissa watched; whatever substance was being applied to dal Nardo's palms, the brush did not come away easily. ''That's a big advantage, any time he gets a grab at you.''

"Then grease me all over, Sparline—except for palms and fingers, of course, and soles of feet. There is more than enough to do it. Quickly, Hawkman—Ernol—help her—for the referee is preparing to call time.''

She felt their hands spread the chilly grease over her; she looked across and saw dal Nardo rise and move forward. He shouted, "What are you doing? Another foul! This wasn't mentioned in the terms.''

"If it wasn't mentioned," said Hawkman, "then certainly it isn't prohibited. Any more than that stuff on *your* hands.''

"Then I, too, will be greased!''

The referee spoke. "Do so, and quickly.''

"I must have it brought.''

"You are limited to what you *did* bring.''

"They have plenty. I demand some of theirs.'' Rissa laughed. Dal Nardo glared, but he said no more.

The referee looked once more at each of them, and made sign to begin. Rissa could not shake hands; she touched fingers to her friends' foreheads and stepped forth.

Dal Nardo stood, waiting. She approached him, so close and no closer; he did not move. She stopped also. Still he made no move. She said, "I see the bull is constipated.''

Then he did move, and it began.

HE rushed like a bull, too—but he needed time to brace himself and launch his great bulk. So, like a matador she waited almost until he reached her, then dove toward and past him—at an angle, her hip grazing his as her right hand clawed for his groin. She felt her nails catch and pull away, too quickly for real damage. But as she rolled and came up facing him, as he turned also, she glanced quickly at her hand and saw his blood.

She looked to dal Nardo; he put a hand to his heavy, loose-hanging scrotum and looked at his stained fingers. The hand shook as he held it out, fingers spread. "I'll reach this into you, and tear out—" Not waiting to hear the rest, she leaped and caught his outstretched thumb in both her hands. Swinging up, braced on his reflex-stiffened arm, she doubled her legs against her belly—then smashed both feet toward his face. She felt one heel slip off to the side but the other caught him squarely, and pushed her up and over. Somersaulting, she kept her grip and felt the thumb give—she let go and landed on her feet, moving backward, almost falling.

Nose gushing blood, dal Nardo charged. He was almost upon her, but she saw the thumb bent to the side and back. She stood fast and chopped at it, then crumpled and rolled directly into his path. The gamble worked; roaring with pain, he tripped and fell over her.

She sprang up to face him, but this time misjudged his speed; he was up and moving toward her. Before she could dodge he backhanded her across the mouth and smashed the edge of his good hand into her side. She fell heavily, and from the pain she knew his blow had cracked or broken a rib—perhaps more than one.

Spitting blood she scrambled, trying to get away and up; she sensed his kick coming and ducked her head but felt something gash her cheek. Desperate now, she rolled again; through the roar of others came Ernol's shout. "The edge! Stay inside!" She scuttled sidewise, away from dal Nardo's looming shadow. Finally she was on her feet; ignoring pain, she feinted a kick at his crotch and—as he faltered—sidestepped, moving away for a moment's respite.

A shout—"Behind you!" Without thought she turned; a hand threw dirt in her face. Coughing, blinded, eyes running tears, she turned and ran—five paces, no more—then turned again and tried to listen for dal Nardo as she knuckled dirt from her eyes. But over the shouting, she could not hear.

"Foul! Hold, dal Nardo! Your man can't get away with that!" Then, blearily, she could see. Splieg stood, huge fist raised like a maul, the other hand against dal Nardo's chest. And she saw Tendal skulking behind dal Nardo's seconds, wiping his hands together.

Without volition her hoarse croak came. "Dig your grave, Blaise Tendal! If I live, you are a dead man!"

Behind her, Ernol shouted, "And if she dies, you're twice dead!"

The referee clapped hands together. "Are you ready?" Splieg gave dal Nardo a final push, making him stagger back a step, then walked out of the circle.

"I am ready," said Rissa, and looked again to dal Nardo. Now he moved more slowly—he had spent his greatest speed —but still he stalked her. A good time to attack, she thought —but her eyes streamed and her breaths came coughing. So she moved in and out, to the sides and back again, feinting and lunging, taking one great blow for every two or three of her lighter ones—and, in balance, losing ground.

Her face ran blood; her side throbbed with pain. Her greased hair had fallen forward, partially, and she could not risk touching it, pushing it back.

She was losing. So she attacked. But first she shouted. "It is time, dal Nardo!" She saw him stiffen, and set her mind to carry out the plan, no matter what it cost her.

A feint to the groin; his good hand countered. Almost at the same time, she stabbed for his eyes and engaged the injured hand. Then she brought her free hand up, backed by a full body lunge, as though the stiff fingers could pierce his throat and emerge behind.

His head jerked to the side; her thrust slipped off the larynx. He grunted and locked his heavy arms around her. Blood trickled from his mouth, and she knew she had not wholly failed. But now his chin was down; she could not reach that spot again.

His voice wheezed. "UET will pay well—I know who you are—*Harnain!* So does Tendal—he'll take word for me—" He coughed blood, but still his crushing grip tightened.

She felt ribs grate—could he live long enough to kill her? And now came the adrenaline effect—time slowed. For as long as lack of breath would allow, she had time to think.

Her hands were free. As hard as she could, she clapped both palms to his ears. But the attempt to kill by concussion failed;

one hand struck before the other. He bellowed—his ears ran blood. She was certain she had deafened him—but in time to save her life?

His nose was flattened and blood-clogged; she thought of stuffing a hand into his panting mouth, against the risk of his teeth. No—there was not time!

She slammed the heel of one hand to the smashed nose—again and again while ribs grated as he bent her backward, trying to break the spine.

Her pointed nails clawed at the side of his neck as she tried for the carotid artery. The skin tore, but blood made the artery too slippery—she could not grasp or pierce it.

Timing the wild shaking of his head, she jammed a thumb into his right eye—his head went back—he shrieked and released her. Then she struck again at the larynx and this time caught it squarely. Twice, while she stood and gasped for breath, dal Nardo hit her. Then he fell. For moments he lay, clutching his throat and kicking feebly. Then he died.

He had dropped her to hands and knees. Now, slowly and with effort, she stood. *One down!* Shaking legs barely supported her as she said, "I have completed the terms of my challenge to Stagon dal Nardo. Now then, Blaise Tendal—"

"No, you don't!" Tendal's voice was shrill. "*I'll* do the challenging here!"

An arm around Rissa kept her from falling again; Felcie Parager said, "You did it—you *did* it! Oh, Tari—I was so frightened for you!" Rissa tried to smile at the girl but was not sure she succeeded.

Then, almost in her ear, Hawkman spoke. "What you'll do, Tendal, is wait your turn. There's another event scheduled here." He and Felcie helped Rissa outside the circle, where the doctor waited to render aid. She sat; someone gave her a drug to dull the pain, and strong drink to sip, and water for her thirst. She was ministered to—creams and solvents cleaned the grease from hair and body; her ribs were taped and her cheek bandaged; blood was wiped from her lips. She lost track of what was done; she sat dazed. After a time she realized that Sparline was trying to explain something.

F. M. Busby

". . . won't take long . . . not committed, after this crisis, unless you want to be. Let's get a robe on you so you look like something *before* the bushstompers got there. All right?"

Confused, Rissa could say only, "I won—I killed him— didn't I?"

"You surely did. But that's past, now. Just stand up and say what's needed." She stood and allowed herself to be robed. Hawkman took her arm again and led her forward a few paces.

He said, "To the assembly I announce a marriage. One party is our victor, Tari Obrigo. The other—" He gestured toward the mask-hooded man. "will not be named publicly at this time. His thumbprint on the certificate is, of course, legal identification."

Tugging at his arm, Rissa whispered, "But I am not wearing the Tari Obrigo prints—not for combat—"

He leaned down to her ear. "So we'll make up another certificate later. This one won't be inspected."

"But why—?"

"It's necessary. Trust me?"

She nodded. "Yes—of course."

Hawkman straightened. "If all is agreed, let us get on with it."

The unnamed man walked to join them; seeing his movements now, Rissa gasped. To Hawkman she said, "But how can *he* be here?"

THE man spoke to her. "Oldstyle or freestyle?"

Hawkman shook his head. "We don't make that distinction here. Now let's begin."

She heard the ritual questions and made her responses by rote. The drugs suppressed her pain but her mind floated, halfway between adrenaline shock and need for rest. At the end, the mask leaned close to her and she kissed the lips, heedless of pain to her own. Then on impulse she clasped the hooded head to her and touched her tongue quickly to the exposed eyelids. "If this is all you will show—" she said—and laughed. Her ribs made her regret it.

"Now if that's all—" Hawkman began, but Blaise Tendal interrupted.

"That's *not* all. I challenge the murderer of Stagon dal Nardo!"

Hawkman tried to hush her but Rissa cried out, "Accepted! I will need five days, I think, to make ready for you. Agreed?" *The UET jackal—if only I could do it now!*

Hawkman clapped his hands, drowning out Tendal's answer. He said, "Your challenge is out of order; you don't have the status. Tari Obrigo is now a Hulzein connection by marriage, so you don't qualify."

"I think I do. I'm a dal Nardo the same way she's a Hulzein. The question's never been decided by review. I demand a hearing!"

A short man, pale of face, rose from where he had helped arrange dal Nardo's body. "You won't need one, Tendal." He looked to Hawkman. "I don't know if you remember me, Moray—I'm Talig dal Nardo, next in line after Stagon. As the new head of the dal Nardos, I declare the marriage between Blaise Tendal and my late brother's daughter null and void."

Red-faced, Tendal threw his hat on the ground and stamped on it. "You frunks! You all hide behind status, don't you? Well, dealing with Blaise Tendal, it won't help you! I'll get her anyway!"

Someone brushed past Rissa; she saw the hood-mask pulled off and tossed aside. But she saw her husband only from behind; she could not see his face as he said, "Tendal! If *I* headed the dal Nardo clan, I'd kill you this minute. If the new head doesn't, he should. Because I'm sure he knows, if you don't, what happens to anyone ever connected with the fool who harms the wife of Bran Tregare!"

SHE watched Tendal's face twist, and thought, *It almost worked—no one could have done it better—but there is no reasoning with a madman*. She did not see how the knife came to Tendal's hand—it flashed toward her; frozen, she looked at death.

A shout—across her view, a hand moved; from it, a blade sprouted. Blood running from his palm, Ernol spun to face her. "Best catch I ever made!"

A ripping, tearing sound clove the air—red steam bloomed from Blaise Tendal's chest and he fell sprawling.

I'm safe now—I'm safe!

The man twitched once and collapsed. The black-robed referee shook the energy-bolt gun to cool it, and said, "I should have done that when he threw the dirt."

BEFORE the doctor could reach him, Ernol pulled the knife from his hand. Wincing, he flexed the bloody fingers. "Lucky —the tendons seem all right."

The doctor looked. "Bleeding's washed it clean. But you'll need a shot—I have to cut a bit, make sure a tendon's not hanging by a thread, ready to pop." Ernol nodded. The work was soon done; then they were ready to leave.

In the aircar Rissa had the back seat to herself, lying down. The extra passengers followed in another car. When they landed, Hawkman and Tregare helped her get out; then she said, "I can walk unaided, I think. Let me?" And they did.

Movement came hard, but she managed it. Tregare stayed close; as they entered the hall he said, "On the ship I took you when I had no right to. Now I've got the right—but I won't come to you until you say so."

She touched his arm, then the tattoo on his cheek. "Be with me now." His brows raised. "No—only to talk—while I soak out some of the hurt in a hot tub."

Liesel, approaching, nodded. "Yes—go with her, Bran. We *all* need to talk, but that can wait." She looked at Rissa. "I've seen you looking prettier, but right now you look damned good to me!" Gently, for a moment she embraced the girl, then turned and said, "Come tell me what happened, will you,

Hawkman? I want to hear all of it.''

The stairs taxed Rissa's waning strength; she leaned on Tregare's arm. In the room she dropped her robe onto a chair. Tregare went ahead and began running water into the tub; she followed him and stood, waiting.

She stared into a mirror. "I look like a gargoyle!" Her lips were grotesquely swollen; blood still oozed from the cuts. Above her bandaged cheek the right eye was swelling and purplish. She touched her upper front teeth and winced. "He's loosened a few. For some days I shall not chew well."

She turned away and cautiously got into the tub, sliding down until only her face appeared above water. She said, "Tregare—in the other room is a brandy flask. Would you pour its cap full for me, please?"

He brought it and she sipped. He sat on a chair beside the tub; for a time, neither spoke. Then he said, "You ever marry before?" Lazily she shook her head, making the water lap against her cheeks. "Neither have I," he said. "It feels . . . odd."

"Do not worry—Sparline said we need not be bound, after this crisis—whatever that may be."

"You don't know? Bleeker on the hook, Fennerabilis still pushing—the oligarchs throwing fits at learning I'm a Hulzein? And now the dal Nardo succession—*that's* not as cut and dried as the little man seems to think, the one that claimed it—"

"Tell me no more, just now—I cannot rouse interest for such things. Say instead how it is that you are here. *Inconnu* was not at the port—did you land elsewhere and travel overland?"

She was kneading lather into her hair. "Here—let me do that." She hitched herself a little higher and let him massage the foam against her scalp. He said, "*Inconnu*'s on her way to orbit one of the outer planets—almost a gray dwarf—about two weeks from here. How I got back—well, armed ships are built to carry scout craft. I used to have two, but one time UET nearly trapped me and I had to use the second as a drone decoy—lost it. Anyway, three days out—past detection range for anything that size—I took the scout and started back.

Came down over the Pole, but somebody spotted me anyway. Landed at a place I have, the other side of the Big Hills, and called Hawkman to come parley.''

"That is where he has been?"

"Right. Now hold your breath and duck your head; this is ready to rinse off." Rubbing briskly, he held her head under until she ran short of air, but lifted it before she needed to resist.

She gasped. "Not so long a submersion next time, please."

He laughed. "Sorry—just being thorough. It's done now."

"So am I, I think." A sudden pain made her wince; she looked at her hand. "I had not noticed, but in the combat I tore my thumbnail."

"Let's see—yes, I'll have to cut it back. And I might as well file down those other claws—we need any more fighting done around here, I'll do it."

"No! The one, yes, but leave the others. No one has to do my fighting for me. And you forget—at least, you did not answer—we are not bound. Sparline said the ceremony was political in purpose."

Trimming the broken nail, he scowled. "Forget politics. The thing is—you want free of me so soon, without even trying the marriage? Without seeing what it's like?"

She looked at him, thinking what it had been like on *Inconnu*. "I cannot know, Tregare, what I will want later. But I recognized you, mask and all, *before* the ceremony, and for now I am in no hurry to dissolve the bond. There will be time for us to decide what we both wish.

"Now—will you help me out of here? My muscles have turned to wax." He grinned, a spontaneous smile that made him look suddenly younger, and aided her to clamber out, and stand. He handed her a large, heavy towel, and with a smaller one began blotting the water from her hair.

Drying herself took longer than usual; each touch found soreness she had not noticed earlier. Tregare finished with her hair; he stood back, and she saw him watching her. She tried to smile, and said, "How can I have such hurt from blows I do not remember?"

He took the towel and helped her into a clean robe. "I don't know—how could anybody your size stand up against dal Nardo and kill the bastard?"

"Dal Nardo was not trained by Erika Hulzein."

His arm around her, they walked into the bedroom. She half sat, half lay on the bed; he took a chair alongside. "Something I didn't know before," he said. "Any day, on *Inconnu*, you could have killed me. The way I treated you, why didn't you?"

She sat up enough to shrug. "At first, because a stranger who kills a captain on his own ship does not long outlive him. Later—as I told you before landing here—I ceased to hate you."

"Ceased to hate? Is that all, Tari?"

Briefly, the realization shocked her—that she had married a man who did not know her name. She shook her head—that question would have to wait. "Oh, more than that, Tregare, but not, probably, what you would like to hear. Toward the end I felt a kind of sympathy, a precarious comradeship—but also, that you were a dangerous man who might still be useful to me."

Blank-faced for a moment, he said, "You still feel that way?"

"After what you said to Tendal before he threw the knife? Ah, no, Tregare—whatever happens between us or does not, I will never try to *use* you. Can you say the same to me?"

His fist pounded into his other palm. "Peace, yes! But I can't speak for the rest of the family. They—"

"They have treated me well—I begrudge no advantage they gained in the course of helping me. I know little of their future plans, but—well, what is *your* opinion?"

"Oh, they'll use you! They—we—use everybody, including each other. In the main, you won't suffer by it—they'll value you the same as the rest of us." Now his laugh was harsh. "But if the stakes are high enough, we're all expendable. *I* sure as peace was."

She leaned toward him, wincing as she put weight on her taped side. "Do you still resent it, that they had to leave you on Earth?"

"I did for so long—maybe I haven't broken the habit. But

I've listened to Hawkman and I believe it—that they had to leave me in hell to save my life.'' He shook his head. ''You wouldn't believe what UET does to young kids, to weed out all but the very toughest. Either you turn into a kind of monster, or you die.''

His eyes looked past her. ''I didn't die, Tari—*I didn't die.*''

She touched his hand. It jerked away from her, then reached back to take hers. ''There—you see? Thinking back to that, any touch—even yours—is a threat.''

''But only for a second—then you recovered quickly enough.''

He shook his head. ''I don't know. It's been years, and still—''

''I know. You have not been able to let go of old hurts. There are methods; I can show you if you like—if you will let me.''

''Maybe—if we ever have time for it—maybe I will.''

''And I—'' But she could not say it aloud. She took her hand away.

''And you, what? Tari?''

Her violent headshake tumbled her hair. ''No—not now, Tregare. I thought of something *I* must do, perhaps. But until I have done it, or failed—'' And why had she never attempted what she knew, in the cause of her own sexuality? Because until now, perhaps, she had not really wished to?

She forced a laugh. ''It is hours short of dinner time, but I have not eaten since morning—and that seems very long ago. I do not want to leave here to dine, anyway, this day. Would you eat with me here, now, or wait and join the others?''

''Here and now's fine. You want me to call and order for us?''

''I would like that. But—'' She touched her swollen mouth. ''—remember, I cannot chew well. Get me soft foods, please.''

He nodded, then spoke over the intercom. Finished, he said, ''Five minutes, maybe ten. All right, Tari?''

''Yes—that long, I can resist starvation.'' She paused, frowning. ''Tregare? As married persons, should we not know one another by our true names?''

"Huh? Oh, yeah—Hawkman mentioned you've been running on a switched ident." He grinned. "That's why that photolock wouldn't open—right? Plastic eyecaps? Funny—I never thought of it, at the time."

"You are right, Tregare; that is how it was." She waited.

He looked at her, then smiled. "You want me to ask, don't you? All right—I'm not married to Tari Obrigo. Who, then?"

"I am sorry it makes little difference to you. To me, it does. I am Rissa Kerguelen. Now, I suppose, we can talk about something else."

His eyes widened; he looked away, at nothing, then back to her. "Sure!" He snapped his fingers. "I remember now—the kid that walked off with twenty million and left UET chasing its own tail. Hey—I was on Earth then, last time I risked that!—trying to promote a hijack, but it didn't work out. Anyway, I *saw* you, on the news!"

"You did?"

"Sure. Blank in the face, at first—bald-headed little dummy, I thought. And then—peace from a pump!—you reared up and told off the whole lot. I loved that! And when you disappeared, that was even better, because the Underground knew UET hadn't caught you." He slapped a palm to one knee. Then his smile went away, and he said, "On the ship —I wish I'd known. I wouldn't have—"

"Ease your mind, Tregare. You did me no damage."

"Maybe not. But still—"

"No. If you are in dire need of something to regret, I am sure we can find a more worthy subject."

"But—well, all right—I—" A knock interrupted him. He answered it, thanked someone and brought the service cart to her bedside. For a few minutes he was busy arranging food on a tray for her. "Soup all right? And fruit paste, and this meat pulped with lerta juice and sour tubers before baking. And some salt-tart pudding—" She did not answer. He fell silent and looked at her. Then he said, "Does my order suit you? Does it—Rissa?"

She nodded. "Yes."

"Real names—if they're important to you, mine is Bran."

"Yes—Bran."

"That's better. Let's eat."

SHE ate slowly—even soup contains ingredients that need chewing—but with enjoyment, shifting the occasional bits of meat or vegetable back to her molars. He finished long before her and sat waiting, saying nothing. Finally she said, "I have had enough. Will you remove the tray, please?" He lifted it back to the cart. "Thank you, Bran."

He made a half smile. "Don't work too hard at it; in a hurry, call me whatever comes to mind. For it's certain I'll do that sometimes; we can't change our thinking all at once."

"Only in private is it important. In public we use our public names automatically; why should this between us be difficult?"

"I don't know—but it's different somehow, isn't it?"

She thought. "Yes, because publicly we use automatic defenses. By ourselves we must discard these or remain strangers. I am glad you have helped me see that difference."

The intercom sounded; he answered on the hushset, then said, "It's Liesel. Wants to know if you're up to a family meeting tonight, or if tomorrow's better."

"Tomorrow—if she will not mind the delay."

He spoke again; then faintly she heard, ". . . tomorrow all right?" and he said, "Maybe breakfast, but I doubt it—midmorning, probably. Yes—good." He cut the circuit and looked to her.

She nodded. "As you put it, is suitable."

"Good. Say—you look tired, and no wonder. You want me out of here?"

"Not unless you wish to go. I am in invalid status, of course, but if you would like merely to *stay* with me, this bed is large, and your presence would comfort me."

"Yes. All right. Maybe yours will comfort me, too."

He leaned toward her. "Not on the lips, Bran—they pain

me too much. The forehead, perhaps?"

"Your nose looks all right, to me."

Then, "Yes—but when you made me laugh, then—my ribs—Bran, I am a ruin!"

"You need sleep. I'll darken the lights."

"Yes." But then she remembered. "There is something first," and she told him what dal Nardo, panting as he strove to kill her, had said of UET—and of payment.

"A UET stringer, was he? I wonder how—but it doesn't matter. Before they can get here, I'll have—never mind, save that for later." Then, after a moment's silence, Tregare said, "Harnain, eh? Not Kerguelen. Simple enough—I haven't entered the data into the computer network yet, but you'll recall how poor Harnain died in a faulty freeze-chamber, on *Inconnu*. That'll take care of anything dal Nardo has on file."

"Yes, it should. Thank you, Bran—and good night."

RISSA heard a noise and halfway woke. Seeing gray dimness at the window, she lay back and dozed again. Later she woke fully, alone in a room filled with daylight. Tentatively she stretched, and felt much soreness but little harsh pain. She lay relaxed, staring at the ceiling but not seeing it.

With no warning knock the door opened; Tregare carried a covered bed-tray. "Good. I thought you'd be awake by now. Here's breakfast." She smiled and thanked him. He said, "And I've done some computer-diddling. Didn't have to use the fake death—Liesel gave me some access-codes, and I've nulled Harnain out of this planet's network."

"Written notes, Bran? Dal Nardo may have had those."

"May have, sure. No more, though—not in his dossier file, anyway. On account of it's melted down to slag."

"What is this you say?"

"Lebeter don't mind a little night work, and he's good with thermite."

"I—I see." Tregare made to lift the food tray's lid but Rissa said, sitting up, "Leave it covered, please, to keep hot until I am back.'' She stood and went into the bathroom. A few minutes later, she returned. "Now, then—I am ready to breakfast with you. And with thanks for all you have done for me.''

"Sure." He nodded. "How's the eye this morning?"

"Better than it appears. I can see with it quite well."

He arranged the tray for her convenience. "I already ate downstairs, but I brought myself an extra coffee cup."

"Did I miss a vital conference?" And looking at the one bowl sitting between containers of juice and coffee, "What is this?"

"Conference? You'll hear it all later. That in the bowl—it's eggs and porridge."

"Eggs *and* porridge? It looks as though a baby might have eaten it once already."

He laughed. "Taste it first—then complain if you like. It's your tender teeth I was looking out for."

From the tip of her spoon she took a wary taste, then nodded. "You are right—despite its appearance, it *is* good. From what is the porridge made?"

"Upland grain, I'm told—from Liesel's holdings across the Big Hills, quite a way south of here. She says there's been a mutation that improved the flavor; she's waiting to see if it breeds true on a commercial scale. Could be a profitable delicacy for the gourmet trade."

"Yes." Until she finished eating she said no more. Then; "Tell me what was said at your breakfast."

"No." He shook his head. "I said, you'll hear it. Once is plenty." He refilled her cup and his own.

"Is something wrong?"

"No. Repetition bores the ears off me—that's all."

She shrugged. "Of course—it is only that I was curious, but I will wait. Well, then—Tregare, there are questions I must ask."

His brows raised. "Tregare, is it, this morning?"

"For these questions, yes."

"Then fire away."

"Tregare—I *want* to accept you. But some things I cannot accept."

"Like what? Peace take you, stop orbiting a dead rock and say what you mean!"

"On *Inconnu* there was the girl Chira. Where is she now? She—"

"Jealous, are you? Climb off it, Tari—Rissa, I mean. I've had others before, and so have you—and we will again, both of us, or I miss my sighting by a lot. What kind of smoke cloud you throwing, anyway?"

"None—as you would know by now, if you would stop interrupting. I am not jealous of Chira past, present or future —I am concerned for her, and for others."

"Others? Who? And *how* are you concerned?"

"For the women on *Inconnu*, who were called property— and for Chira, that she might become one of them. Tregare— I do not condone slavery, of any kind. Under the guise of Total Welfare I have *been* a slave. I—"

He laughed, and she saw his relief was real. "Oh—for the love of peace! All right—I admit I used that property thing to throw a fright into Chira when she needed one. She's a barbarian—literally—I picked her up on a backslid colony planet and her tribe was the *outcasts* of the whole sorry lot."

"Then why did you want her?"

"I bought her, if you have to know—for a packet of drug-sticks and a rusty knife—because she was next up for sacrifice to their tribal god, who seemed to be a pretty nasty bastard as such things go. So I washed her up and moved her in with me, since she didn't fit anywhere else on the ship—and one thing and another led to where you might expect. But she's a gutsy wench—threw tantrums for any reason or none—destructive as hell. I needed something to keep her in line."

"Then the—property thing—it was all fiction?"

"No—not all." He frowned and gestured to her. "Wait a minute—to make sense to you, I'll have to go back a little."

She sipped cool coffee. "Go back as far as you like."

"All right. I was groundside—it doesn't matter where— when a UET ship landed, and I got to drinking with its captain. Hoped to find a way to take the ship, but I didn't have enough men and weapons to do it. And his ship was unarmed, so he couldn't do anything about *me*, so we had a truce. Well, the man talked, and I got another idea.''

"As yet there are no women in this story."

"Sure there are—nearly fifty of them, on that ship as cargo. And they *were* property—UET's. Female Welfare clients, consigned to a UET mining world that's twelve men to every woman—to be sold there and kept in cribs to service the miners. Like you said—slaves.''

"And *your* idea, Tregare?''

"You're calling me that to needle me, right? Well, never mind, for now. All right—I bought those women, traded for them, while that skipper was drunk. Now, before you holler— some of the Hidden Worlds are short of women, too, and they'll pay—but for *free* women, no slavery.'' He paused. "Well, there was for a while, on one planet. But the *Buonatierra* landed there and killed a few people that needed it, and the rest changed their ways.''

"This is more than I need to know about places that do not concern us. What of the women on *Inconnu?*''

"Yeah—well, they were just cargo, in a way. Rode cramped —but clean, and fed decently—best I could do. And nobody touched them—except my medics, in line of duty. You have to know, they came aboard filthy and stinking—raw sores that'd make you puke. Lots better shape they were in, when they got off.''

"Oh? They have disembarked? Where, may I ask?''

"*Here*! Where else could they?''

"And what has happened to them?''

"We all got lucky. You know the other ship at the port when I took off? Quinlan's *Red Dog*—next port of call, Farmer's Dell—a colony that needs women, can pay, and treats them right. It's a long haul but Quinlan's freeze-chambers work. I made expenses and a little better on the deal, and I don't expect Quinlan will lose on it, either.''

"So instead of a slaver, Tregare, you are a great benefactor?''

He glared at her. "I told you the truth; what more do you want?''

"Where is the girl Chira?''

"On her way, with the rest.''

"With or without her consent?"

"I told her how it was; she decided for herself. That's truth. Fucked me a good one, too—insisted on it, in fact—before she got off. That suit you, or do you still think I lie to you?"

Rissa smiled. She shook her head. "Bran Tregare, you are too proud to lie—except, of course, in the line of business. No—" She reached her hands toward him. "—you are what my father used to say—a brass-plated sonofabitch who takes no crap from *anyone*. There is much to be said for that kind of person. So I accept you . . .

"No—not *yet*, you ravisher of cripples!" But she was laughing and his hands were gentle on her, and her lips did not pain greatly as she kissed him. Then he rose and sat again, grave-faced and watching her.

"Rissa—can you fit into the stretched-out life I must lead?"

"How could I know? But for now, while we are here, I think I can. Shall we try?"

He smiled, and she said, "Before facing your family, I need another soak, another hot tub. Help me?" He did, and when she lay with only eyes, nose and mouth above the steaming water, she said, "Bran Tregare—now I shall trust you."

"If you do," he said, "then except for my people on *Inconnu*, you'll be the first."

LATER, dried and dressed, she looked in the mirror and shook her head—makeup would not hide the great plum-colored bruise of her eye and cheek. She brushed her still-damp hair back to hang straight, and joined Tregare in the bedroom. "I am ready."

Starting down the stairs, soreness caught at her muscles, but the brief exercise soon eased them. They found Liesel in her office, frowning over a sheet of figures. She said, "Up and around, are you? That eye takes first prize, but you move well enough. How do you feel?"

"Stiff—sore—but nothing serious. Already my teeth are more solid and pain me less." Liesel looked puzzled; Rissa pointed. "These in front—dal Nardo's backhand nearly removed them. But they will be all right."

"Good. Here—sit, you two. I'm trying to figure dal Nardo's net personal worth—his estate's, I mean—and the readout on his public records is peace's own mess."

Rissa frowned. "Dal Nardo's estate? Why?"

"To figure your share. Didn't you know about that? Having dueled him to death, all legal and proper, you get a third of it."

"No one told me before. Will it be any great amount, do you think?"

Tregare laughed. "He'll have most of it squirreled away in trusts and under dummies. The trick is to nose it out."

"Which will cost you ten percent commission, Rissa. All right?"

"Of course, Liesel. I do not yet know enough about your especial legalities here, to do it myself. Perhaps I can sit with you and learn?"

"Sure. Or, better yet, why not wait until I'm done, and we can go over it together in summary?"

"Certainly," Rissa paused. "Liesel, you are being very businesslike—and in my interests, to my benefit—but I am afraid I do not feel at all that way, myself. I—" Tears began to come; she blinked them away.

Liesel rose and grasped her arm. "Girl—something's wrong?" Rissa shook her head. "Good—there shouldn't be. After all—you won your fight, saved your life and status with honor. And your share of dal Nardo's holdings—not to mention the bet with Bleeker—you won't be one of the smaller frogs in the oligarchal puddle. You—" She looked closely at Rissa. "So why are your eyes leaking like a pair of cracked cups?"

"Because—none of that—it is not what is *important* to me now!" She gripped Tregare's hand and put her other arm around Liesel's neck, pulling the two close to her.

"Then in the name of peace," said Liesel, "what *is* important?"

Face muffled against Liesel's shoulder, she said, "When I was five years old, they killed my parents and put me into

Welfare. I had forgotten what it was like to have a family, to be a part of it. Ever since I was a little girl—and now I see, that in some ways I still am one—I have been alone. But now—"

As Tregare's free hand stroked her hair and cheek, she heard Liesel say, "Well, *of course* you've got a family now! You're a Hulzein by marriage, aren't you? Nothing less—and you fought your way in, earned it!" As much as hearing Liesel's laugh, against her face and body Rissa felt it.

"Little girl? No such thing." In Liesel's voice, for a moment Rissa heard Erika's. "You've a way to go—we all have —but you're growing up, young Rissa!"